REPRISAL

William W. Johnstone

The Last Gunfighter:
REPRISAL

WHEELER
PUBLISHING, INC.
ROCKLAND, MA

★ AN AMERICAN COMPANY ★

Published in large print by arrangement with Pinnacle Books, an imprint of Kensington Publishing Corp., in the United States and Canada.

Wheeler Large Print Book Series.

Set in 16 pt Plantin.

Library of Congress Cataloging-in-Publication Data

Johnstone, William W.
    Reprisal / William W. Johnstone.
       p. (large print) cm. (Wheeler large print book series)
    ISBN 1-58724-195-1 (softcover)
    1. Fathers and sons—Fiction. 2. Kidnapping—Fiction. 3. Colorado—Fiction. 4. Large type books. I. Title. II. Series.

[PS3560.O415 R47 2002]
813'.54—dc21
                                    2002016793
                                              CIP

The only thing necessary for the triumph of evil is for good men to do nothing.

Edmund Burke

One

Frank Morgan drifted into Denver and checked into a hotel, signing the register F. Morgan. The desk clerk never so much as raised an eyebrow.

Frank had dropped out of sight after leaving the mining town now officially renamed Crossing. The town would slowly fade into oblivion, and shortly after the turn of the century would cease to exist.

But Denver was booming and would continue to grow.

Frank had himself a bath and haircut and shave, and bought some new clothes, including a new hip-length jacket, for the nights were turning colder as late fall began settling over the high country.

Frank found a small cafe and ordered coffee as he looked over the rather sparse offerings on the menu, finally waving the tired-looking waitress over and ordering the special.

"It ain't nothin' special," she told him. "But it'll fill you up."

"That's what I need, ma'am," Frank replied. "For I'm sure tired of eating my own cooking."

"Been on the trail long?"

"Long enough so that it took two fills in the bathhouse to get the fleas off me."

She laughed at that. "I'll get your food right out to you."

"Thanks."

Frank sipped his coffee while waiting for his food. His weeks on the lonesome had been quiet ones, with no trouble, and that was the way he liked it. But no trouble for Frank Morgan was about to come to an end. He had gotten a line on the newly formed gangs of Ned Pine and Victor Vanbergen, and it was not a pretty picture the people he had talked with had painted in his mind.

Ned and Vic and their gangs had been reported raiding all over the West during their careers that spanned about eight or ten years, but mostly in a three-state area: Colorado, Wyoming, and Montana. They were cold-blooded killers, the last of the big outlaw gangs still working as the West was slowly settling down. It was still wild and woolly and full of fleas, but very slowly civilization was tightening its grip.

But their fatal mistake was in killing the only woman Frank had ever loved: Vivian Browning. For that, the Pine and Vanbergen gangs would pay the price...every damned one of them, right down to the last man.

It had gotten back to Frank that the gang members all boasted and laughed about the killing of Vivian as if it were a big joke. Whenever Frank allowed himself to think about that, it filled him with a terrible deadly coldness. When he finished with the gang, none would be alive to laugh at anything else. He struggled to push those thoughts from him, and succeeded only with an effort.

The waitress placed his food in front of him, refilled his coffee cup, and left him alone. Frank dug in. The food was not fancy, but it was good and filling, and the bread was fresh-baked and hot.

He cleaned his plate and waved at the waitress for more coffee. Then he rolled a cigarette and sat for a time, staring out the window at the goings-on in the busy street and on the boardwalk.

Denver was a fast-growing city, too damn big for Frank's liking. Too many laws and rules. Why, a man couldn't even tote a gun around in Denver...not legally anyway. But regardless of what the law stated, Frank carried a short-barreled .45 in a shoulder rig, hidden under his coat. He suspected that he was not alone in carrying a concealed weapon.

Frank finished his coffee, left a tip on the table for the pleasant and very attentive waitress, paid his bill at the counter, and exited the cafe. There was a cold wind blowing, a reminder that winter was just around the corner.

Frank stood for a time on the boardwalk, checking things out before he started walking. Frank Morgan, a man whom the press had recently begun calling The Drifter, was one of the few fast guns still alive in the West. There were others certainly: Smoke Jensen, Louis

Longmont...but that was about it. All the rest were either dead or retired, but there were others just as fast, or faster, who had not yet made a name for themselves. It was those that Frank had to watch out for, for those who fancied themselves gunslicks were hunting a name, and they were ruthless and persistent in hunting down and bracing the few really fast guns still alive.

Frank had a job to do, and he was single-minded about it. He didn't have either the time or the inclination to deal with some trouble-hunting punk.

Frank Morgan was a shade over six feet tall. He was broad-shouldered and lean-hipped, a very muscular man. He was in his mid-forties, and had carried the title of gun-fighter ever since he was fifteen years old and forced into a gunfight with an older man down in Texas. Frank had killed the man, and several years later had been forced into a wild gunfight with the man's brothers. Frank had killed them all.

His reputation as a gunfighter was set in stone on that day.

That was many years and many, many gun-fights ago. Frank's number of dead men left behind him could not equal that of Smoke Jensen, nor did he want it to, but nonetheless, his numbers were staggeringly high. Frank had not started a single one of those fights, but he had finished them all.

Frank had married here in Denver, a lovely girl named Vivian, but her father, a wealthy

4

man, hated Frank and framed him for a crime he didn't commit, then said he would not pursue it if Frank would leave and never see Vivian again. Frank had no choice; he pulled out, and didn't see or hear from Vivian for years.

Her father had the marriage annulled.

Vivian remarried and took over her father's many businesses after his death, and became one of the wealthiest women in America. Vivian's husband had died a few years back. She had a son, Conrad, and it was not until a few months back that Frank discovered the young man was his own son.

It came as quite a shock.

Frank had drifted into a mining town in northern New Mexico and discovered that Vivian was there, overseeing a huge mining operation. But a few weeks later, after Frank and Vivian had begun to pick up the pieces and get back together, Vivian was dead, killed by the Pine and Vanbergen gangs.

Frank swore to track down and destroy the gangs.

Even if it took him the rest of his life.

Frank walked slowly back to his hotel, and in the lobby paused to buy a newspaper before going to his room. He had not read a newspaper in several months and was hungry for news.

But there wasn't a whole lot going on, according to this newspaper.

This paper was endorsing Benjamin Harrison for President. The election was going to be held in a few weeks. Frank didn't think he would vote. He wasn't at all sure he could vote, since he didn't have a permanent address... although he didn't think that made much difference, since a great many politicians stressed the theme "Vote early and often."

There was something going on about Chinese laborers in America. Something called the Scott Act. Frank wasn't sure what all that was about either.

Harrison said that if elected President he would open that part of Indian Territory known as Oklahoma for settlement and that United States land laws would be in force.

Frank folded the newspaper and laid it aside. There had been no mention of the Pine and Vanbergen gangs, and that was all Frank was interested in. But one news item had caught his attention: a gold strike in an area west and slightly north of Denver. A big gold strike. Frank decided to ride in that direction in a couple of days; check it out.

He heard the rumble of thunder and glanced out the window. The first few splatterings of raindrops pocked the window that faced the street. Frank always enjoyed sleeping in a real bed when it rained. It was comforting to him, always lulling him into a gentle sleep. It had been several months since he'd slept in a real bed with a roof over his head.

He made sure the door was securely locked, as secure as it could be with a skeleton key, and just to be extra safe, he wedged a chair under the doorknob.

Frank tugged off his boots and placed them

by the bed. He stretched out, head on the pillow, and closed his eyes. It was not yet cold enough to build a fire in the small stove, but with the unpredictability of the high country weather this time of the year, it might be, later on in the night.

The rain did not lull Frank into a peaceful, dreamless sleep. His sleep brought a jumble of unpleasant dreams.

He dreamt of many of the men who had faced his gun and died for their folly. There was that kid in Kansas in that little no-name town right after the war. Billy something or another, about eighteen or so. Frank had tried to warn the kid off, had done his best to walk away from him, but Billy had insisted on forcing his hand.

Billy died on the dirty floor of the saloon that night. He hadn't even cleared leather before Frank's bullet tore into his heart.

There was that older man in Arizona, one afternoon years ago, who called Frank out into the street in the mistaken belief that Frank had killed his brother. Frank repeatedly told the man he'd never heard of the man's brother and to go away and leave him alone, but the man persisted, cursing Frank and calling him yellow. Seconds later the man went for his gun and in a single heartbeat, the man was gut-shot, writhing in pain and dying in the street. Frank turned away, mounted up, and rode out of town.

Then the dream about the father and his sons came to haunt him again. Frank had stopped off in a small blot on the map in the panhandle of Texas for supplies. There was a liquored-up young man in the general store/trading post/saloon. The young man had a bad mouth and an evil temper. He braced Frank and Frank tried to ignore him, but the punk kept pushing and pushing, and finally he put hands on Frank.

Frank didn't like for people to put hands on him. He flattened the young man with a big hard right fist and left him addled on the floor.

Someone yelled for Frank to watch out. Frank turned, his .45 leaping into his hand. The punk had leveled a .44 at him, hammer back.

Frank shot him right between the eyes and made a big mess on the floor behind the young man's head.

The young man's father and his other two sons caught up with Frank on the trail about a week later.

The father and his sons didn't believe in much conversation. They opened fire on Frank as soon as they got within range. Frank headed for an upthrusting of rocks and brush and an all-day battle ensued. The father and one of his sons were killed, the remaining son badly wounded. Frank patched up the wounded man as best he could, buried the other two, and pulled out. There was nothing else he could do.

He dreamed of the time he found a family butchered by Indians. Frank was prowling through the ruins of the cabin when a small posse from a nearby town rode up, and in their ugly rage thought Frank had committed the atrocity. That was a very ugly scene, involving a hanging rope...until Frank filled both hands with Colts and made a believer out of the sheriff and what remained of his posse after the very sudden, explosive, and bloody shootout. Frank carefully avoided the north-western part of Arizona for several years after that.

Frank fought himself out of sleep and the exhausting dreams, and sat on the edge of the bed for a moment, gathering his thoughts. He hated it when those dreams entered his sleep, and often wondered just what they meant...or if they meant anything at all.

He had slept fitfully for several hours. It was full dark. Frank popped a match into fire and lit the lamp by the side of the bed. He pulled on his boots, filled the water basin, and washed the sleep out of his eyes. He but-toned up his shirt, slipped into his shoulder-holster rig, and pulled on his coat. He needed several cups of good strong coffee. Maybe that would put him into a better frame of mind. Maybe he could find a friendly poker game. Frank occasionally enjoyed a low-stakes game of cards with players who knew how and when to bet and when to toss it in, and didn't lose control of their tempers when they lost.

He had to find something to do, for he cer-tainly wasn't sleepy.

He ran his fingers through his thick dark-brown hair, peppered with some gray, and made a mental note to buy a comb or a brush when the stores opened in the morning. Then he popped the cover on his pocket watch and checked the time. Nine o'clock. He had sure slept more than a few hours. He stood looking at his image in the slightly warped mirror and grimaced, thinking it was going to be a long night. He automatically checked his short-barreled .45 and shoved it back into leather, then slipped the chair from under the doorknob, unlocked the door, and stepped out into the hall.

He checked the hotel dining room. Closed. He stepped out onto the boardwalk and into the cold night air.

"Morgan," the voice called out of the darkness from his right.

"That's me," Frank said.

"I don't mean no harm," the voice said. "So don't get nervous and haul no iron."

"I'm listening."

"The ante's done went up on your head, Morgan. Somebody really wants to see you dead. They's ten thousand dollars to the man who kills you."

"Interesting. Who's putting up the money?"

"Somebody from back East is what I hear. Boston, I think. Some lawyer feller."

"Dutton."

"That's him! Yeah."

"Why are you telling me this?"

"You done me a favor once. Long time ago."

10

"Oh?"

"Yeah. I was drunk and mouthy and real pushy. You didn't kill me. You just walked away and let me live. I ain't never forgot that."

"I appreciate it, friend."

"Forget it. I'm gone, Morgan. Watch your back."

"I'll do that."

The unknown man walked away, his boots clumping on the boardwalk.

Frank stood in the cold wind for a moment. Ten thousand dollars was a lot of money. And it would bring out any number of man-hunters.

"Wonderful," he muttered. "That's all I need."

A policeman walked by and gave Frank the once-over. Frank stared right back, as was his habit. The policeman stopped and looked squarely at Frank.

"Something on your mind, officer?" Frank asked.

"You look familiar to me, that's all. You ever been in Denver before?"

"Not since it got this big."

The officer smiled. "It has grown, hasn't it?"

"It's a regular city."

"Passin' through?"

"On my way into the mountains to the strike. Probably pull out in the morning."

"Way I hear it, it's a big one. I've heard of nuggets big as your fist found up there." The officer smiled. "Course, now, I haven't seen any of those. Well, good luck to you." The policeman touched his hat. "Take it easy."

"Thank you. I will."

Frank wandered for a couple of blocks until coming to a saloon. The batwings were pulled back and the front door was closed to keep out the cold wind. Frank stepped inside and stood for a moment, eyeballing the scene. A few men stood at the long bar, drinking alone. About half the tables were filled. Frank walked to the bar and ordered a whiskey. No one paid him more than a cursory glance.

Frank lingered over his drink for a time. He was not much of a drinking man, but did occasionally enjoy a whiskey. The talk was about the recent strike up in the mountains, and if one were to believe even half of what was being said, it was indeed a very big strike.

Frank perked up and listened more carefully when someone said, "And wouldn't you know it? Henson Enterprises has staked out half of the area, and already they own the biggest and best-producing mine."

"Is that squirt kid who lived here in town for a time running it? The one who took over the company after his mother was killed down in New Mexico?"

"You bet he is. Cocky little bastard too."

Conrad Browning. Frank's son.

Conrad had escorted his mother's body back East, then returned to the West to oversee the company's business, even though he had told Frank he hated the West and would never return. How interesting.

12

"You know what? I hear tell that snooty kid is really Frank Morgan's son."

"Are you serious? The gunslick Morgan?"

"That's what I keep hearin'."

"Well, roll me in buffalo crap and call me stinky. How in the hell did something like that happen?"

"Beats me. But that's the talk goin' around."

"You believe it?"

"I kinda do. After hearing 'bout what happened down at that little town in New Mexico..."

Frank stopped listening and stared down into the amber liquid in his shot glass. So Conrad was running the show in the mountains. Seeing him again should be interesting, since the young man did not much like Frank...and that was being kind, considering Conrad's real feelings toward his biological father.

Frank finished his drink and walked slowly back to the hotel. He wouldn't have to travel far to find the Pine and Vanbergen gangs. Gold would draw them like a powerful magnet. Frank would provision up and pull out in the morning.

The police were waiting for him when he got back to the hotel.

Two

"Frank Morgan?" one of the uniformed officers asked.

"That's me," Frank replied.

"What's your business in Denver, Morgan?" another asked.

"Passing through."

"To where?"

"Beats me. I'm just drifting."

"Might be best if you just drifted on out of this town."

"Oh, I plan to do just that. First thing in the morning."

The two officers stared at Frank for a moment. The first officer said, "No offense meant, Morgan. But gunfighters are not welcome in this town."

"No offense taken," Frank replied easily. "I'd hate to run into a gunfighter myself."

Both police officers smiled at that. The second officer said, "Keep your guns in leather while you're here, Morgan. For your own good."

"I plan to."

"Good luck to you."

"Thanks."

Frank sat in the lobby for a long time after the officers left. *If I had any sense at all,* he thought, *I'd stop this plan of revenge and head on to California and start a new life while I have time. If I kill all of the Pine and Vanbergen gangs, that won't bring Viv back.*

But, he thought with almost an audible sigh, *even though Conrad doesn't want my help, he's still my son, and I owe him any help I can give him.*

Frank also had a hunch that this gold strike was just about it for that area. Many, many millions of dollars in gold had been mined out of the area since 1860, and now that silver prices had been going up, and new lodes of silver found, Central City and Black Hawk and the other gold-mining towns and camps in the area would soon see a rapid decline. Frank had seen it all before, many times.

He went up to his room and stretched out on the bed. He didn't think he would sleep, but when he opened his eyes and lit the lamp to check his watch, it was almost five o'clock in the morning.

"A man could get used to a feather bed," Frank muttered.

He finished his morning toilet quickly, and was packed up and ready to go in fifteen minutes. The hotel dining room was open. Frank opted for a couple of cups of coffee, which was a tad on the weak side for his taste.

He sat in the lobby until the darkness was slowly pushed away by a dim gray light, then picked up his saddlebags and rifle and walked over to the livery. His horses were glad to see him, and appeared anxious to once more get on the trail.

He saddled up his riding horse, cinched down the packsaddle, and headed out of Denver. He stopped at a small store on the edge of town and bought bacon, beans, flour, and coffee. Then he bought several boxes of ammunition for his pistols and his .44-40 rifle.

He lashed down his supplies, covered them with a tarp, and mounted up. He would take his time going to the mining camp, as yet the place had no name and probably never would.

"Mister." The store clerk hailed him from the boardwalk just as Frank was lifting the reins.

Frank paused and looked at the man.

"You headin' out for the new gold camp?"

"I was thinking about it."

"Be careful. Outlaws workin' that area hot and heavy. There ain't no law up there either."

"The Pine and Vanbergen gangs?"

"You've heard about them, hey?"

"A little."

"Yep. That's the bunch that's raisin' all sorts of hell up in the mountains. Packs of vicious white trash, that's what they are."

Frank smiled. "You from the South, mister?"

"You bet. Alabamy originally. I come out here with my folks right after the war. Goddamn Yankees burnt ever'thin' we owned. I still hate 'em. You?"

"Texas."

"You be careful, Texas. And watch out for them outlaws, you hear?"

"I hear. Thanks."

Frank rode slowly out of town. Once past the city-limits sign, he stopped and took off his shoulder rig, stowing it in his saddlebags, and belted on his pistol, a Colt .45 Peacemaker.

16

On the left side of his gunbelt, he carried a long-bladed sheath knife, honed to razor sharpness.

Back in the saddle, he pressed on, heading for the mountains that loomed ahead. It was a good two-day ride to the mining camp, but Frank was in no hurry. If it took a week, that was fine with him.

The mountain road was narrow, in most places barely wide enough for two wagons to pass. There were pull-off places cut out for wagons to pull over and wait for an approaching wagon to get clear.

At noon, Frank stopped for a lunch of crackers and cheese and a pickle he'd bought back at the general store on the edge of town, and to let his horses blow and roll. He washed his lunch down with cold water from a fast-rushing stream, and then rolled a cigarette and relaxed. He longed for a cup of good strong coffee, but he had a case of the lazies: He didn't feel like digging out the pot and building a fire.

Several huge wagons rumbled by in a group, under heavy guard by mounted outriders, front and back. Frank counted a dozen heavily armed men on horseback, and the drivers and guards on the wagons were all well armed. They did not wave at Frank, and the mounted men gave him stern looks and suspicious once-overs as they rode past.

"Howdy to you too, boys," Frank muttered. "Nice day, isn't it?"

The wagons rumbled on out of sight and sound, heading for Denver.

Frank stood up and stretched a couple of

times, getting the kinks out of his muscles, and then saddled up and cinched up both animals. He was just about to climb into the saddle when four men rode into view, coming up the trail. They had been about forty-five minutes behind Frank. Frank immediately formed an opinion of the duster-wearing quartet: He didn't like them.

Frank always trusted his initial hunches...at least until the subject or subjects in question proved him wrong.

And that didn't occur very often.

The approaching men were well mounted. Frank couldn't tell how well armed they were because of the long trail dusters they wore, but he suspected they were heavily armed. The closer they came, the more Frank's suspicions grew.

Frank retrieved his short-barreled .45 from a saddlebag and slipped it into the left-side pocket of his jacket. His jacket was unbuttoned and he brushed the right side back, clearing his Peacemaker for a draw.

The quartet slowed as they approached Frank. Frank watched as they all slowly unbuttoned their long dusters, clearing the way for a draw.

"That pretty well tells the story," Frank muttered. "Bounty hunters. Out to pick up the ten thousand dollars that's on my head."

The four men stepped their horses off the road and lined up to face Frank. They stared at him in silence for a long moment, then carefully dismounted, taking care never to turn their backs on Frank Morgan.

Frank stepped away from his horse and walked to his right a few paces. The stream was behind him, a solid wall of upward-jutting rock on the other side of the fast-moving mountain creek. A few more yards to his right, there was scrub brush and a pile of rock from the carving out of the roadway. Frank figured he had a chance to make the cover of those rocks...maybe.

"Frank Morgan?" one of the men called.

"Who wants to know?" Frank responded.

"That ain't important," another of the quartet said. "You was asked a question, so answer it."

"Why don't you go to hell?" Frank told him.

The questioner frowned and flushed darkly. "It's Morgan," he said. "Smart mouth and all."

"Has to be," another man agreed.

"He shore don't look like much to me," the fourth member of the group remarked.

Frank smiled at that.

"You think I said somethin' funny, Morgan?" the man asked.

"I think you're a fool," Frank told him.

"Bastard," the man muttered.

"You boys think ten thousand dollars is worth dying for?" Frank asked.

"Huh?" the first man that had spoken, said. "Ten thousand?"

The other three got a good laugh out of that.

"You way behind the times, Morgan. The ante's done been raised to fifteen thousand."

"I guess somebody must really hate me to offer that much money. Either that or they're really afraid of me. Which one is it, boys?"

"Don't know, don't care."

"Then make your play and let's get this dance started."

"You in that big a hurry to die, Morgan?"

"I have no intention of dying," Frank told him. "What's bothering me is what I'm going to do with your bodies. Ground around here is too damn rocky to dig in."

The four men exchanged quick glances.

"I guess I'm just going to have to leave you here on the ground and let the buzzards eat your innards."

"You got nerve, Morgan," the man who appeared to be the boss said. "I'll give you that much. But I think you're a fool to boot. Just in case you can't add, let me sum it up for you: There's four of us and only one of you."

"That's right, Hog Face, but when one of you makes a move to pull on me, I'll kill two of you before the others can clear leather."

"Hog Face!"

"That's what I said. I call it like I see it, and you look like a hog to me. You are just about the ugliest thing I ever did see."

"Why...damn you to hell, Morgan!"

"You could hire that face of yours out to scare little children."

Hog Face flushed with anger, but made no move to drag iron. The other three exchanged nervous glances. This was not going as they had been told it would. They had been told that Frank Morgan was an old man who had lost his nerve and his speed.

The bounty hunters suspected that someone had lied to them.

"Go home, boys," Frank said softly, his words just carrying to the four men. "Give this up."

"Give up fifteen thousand dollars, Morgan?" Hog Face replied. "I don't think so."

"Then let's get it going," Frank said. He jerked iron and shot Hog Face in the belly.

Three

Hog Face doubled over in shock when the .45 bullet slammed into him. His pistol dropped back into his holster and he went down to one knee in pain, both hands clutching his perforated belly.

Frank fired as he ran for the protection of the rocks, one round missing his target, the second round knocking a leg out from another bounty hunter.

Frank jumped into the rocks just as the lead began howling all around him.

Hog Face was out of it. He was stretched out full length on the ground, his life's blood slowly leaking out. The man with the broken leg was crawling away, toward the roadbed, his pistol on the ground where he'd dropped it, the battle forgotten, at least for the moment.

"Lloyd?" someone tossed out. "Are you alive?"

"He's bad hit," the man with the broken leg called, slipping behind a mound of dirt and rocks. "And so am I. Can't stop the bleedin'."

"Hang on," the other man called. "I'm on my way."

He didn't make it.

The bounty hunter jumped up, and Frank drilled him before he had taken five steps. The .45 slug tore into his left side and blew out the right side. The man dropped like a rock and slowly rolled down the slight incline.

The fourth man made a fast run for his horse. Keeping the animal between himself and Frank's gun, the bounty hunter made the road, and was gone without another glance back at the bloody carnage that once was his buddies. He headed down the road, toward the Denver junction.

Frank reloaded before exiting the rocks. Pistol in his hand, he walked over to Hog Face. He was unconscious and dying. Frank carefully edged over to the man he'd dusted side to side. He was stone dead.

"You got to hep me, Morgan!" the third bounty hunter hollered. "I'm bleedin' bad."

"That's your problem," Frank said, walking over to him. "You boys wanted this shootout, not me."

"Fifteen thousand dollars is a powerful lot of money, Morgan. You can't blame us for that."

"The hell I can't!"

"You gonna leave me here?"

"What do you want me to do, tote you to a doctor?"

"That'd be white of you, yeah."

Frank knelt down beside the man. His bullet had torn the big vein in the leg. Frank rigged a tourniquet on the wound and stood up.

"That's it?" the wounded man said. "That there is all you're gonna do?"

"That's about it, bounty hunter."

"That's cold, Morgan. Mighty damn cold of you."

"I reckon so."

"I'll kill you someday, Morgan. I promise you that."

Frank had heard that threat many times over the long years. "What's your name?"

"Jake Miller. And I got kin too."

"Good for you." Frank turned away and started to walk off.

"They'll git you, Morgan."

"They'll try."

Jake cussed him.

Frank tossed all the pistols he could find into the stream, then gathered up his animals and swung into the saddle.

"Don't leave me here to die, you bastard!" Jake yelled. "That ain't decent."

"Decent?" Frank looked down at the man. "What the hell would you know about decency?"

Frank rode off without saying another word or looking back. Jake cussed him until he was out of sight.

Frank rode into the mining camp the next day. What buildings there were in the town were raw, the smell of fresh-cut lumber strong. It was not a smell that was new to Frank. Nor was the sight of the crowded streets new. He had smelled and seen it all before, many times.

The largest and newest building on Main Street had a sign that read: The Henson Company.

Frank bought a few supplies at a general store. He didn't bother inquiring at the only hotel. He knew it would be packed, men sleeping four or five to a room. He rode on out of town and turned down a rutted road that led off to the south. He had usually been able to find a deserted cabin or shack close to these boom-towns, and this time was no exception. He had ridden about two miles, away from the strike area, which was about three miles north of the town, when he came to a fairly decent-looking cabin that appeared to be deserted. There was a lean-to in the rear. He looked inside the cabin. It was bare except for a small stove and a bunk in the main room that was built against the wall.

"Good enough for me," Frank muttered.

Frank checked the lean-to. Someone had left several bales of hay stacked in one corner.

"Nice of them," Frank said.

Walking around the cabin, Frank discovered

a pile of firewood. He wouldn't have to cut any wood for several weeks...if he stayed around that long, which he doubted.

After forking some hay into the two stalls of the lean-to, Frank stripped the load off the packhorse, pulled the saddle off his riding horse, and stabled both his horses. Then he began settling in.

He found a broken-handled broom and swept out the cabin, then cleaned the stove and built a fire for coffee. He paused at a strange sound coming from the outside, then went out to check and found a dog sitting on the ground.

Frank didn't know what kind of dog it was. It was just a dog. Mixed breed...very mixed. It was brown and coarse-haired like a wolf. It wasn't a very big dog. Frank figured it weighed about thirty pounds. It didn't appear to be very old, maybe two or three years.

"What's the matter, boy," he said, squatting down, taking care not to sit on his spurs and jab himself in the butt. "Your people leave you behind?"

The dog wagged its tail.

Frank held out a hand and the animal came to him cautiously. Frank petted the animal for a moment. The dog was sure enough friendly. Probably glad to see someone who didn't throw rocks at it or yell at it. "You hungry, boy?"

The dog wagged its tail furiously.

"I reckon you are. All right, well, come on in and I'll fix us both something to eat."

The dog hesitated, then followed Frank into the cabin. Frank fried up some bacon and then made pan bread, and he and the dog ate it all up. Frank poured himself a cup of coffee, and sat down on the unmade bunk and watched as the dog finished up the bread.

"Well, I guess you had a name. But somebody forgot to tell me. So I guess I'll just call you Dog. How's that, fellow?"

The dog looked at him and wagged his tail. "Dog it is."

Frank drank his coffee and watched as Dog scratched himself...several times. And that got Frank scratching himself.

"This won't do," Frank muttered, rising from the bunk. He went outside, Dog following, and began looking around. He found a wooden bucket with a broken handle and a large metal pot in a pile of junk in back of the shed. "You're going to have a bath," he told Dog.

He filled the bucket with water from the creek several times and toted it inside, filling up the large metal pot. He stoked up the fire in the old cookstove and while the water heated, he got a large bar of soap from his supplies.

Dog sensed what was about to happen and hit the trail. It took Frank about fifteen minutes to coax him back and get a rope on him. "Now you get a bath, Dog."

By the time Frank finished, they both had gotten a bath. But Dog was free of fleas...at least for the time being.

Frank fixed Dog a place to sleep in a corner of the room and pointed to it. "You sleep there," he told the animal.

Dog looked at him, and promptly dragged

the old blanket to a place under the bunk and lay down.

"All right," Frank said, laughing. "I won't argue with you. Stay put."

Frank fixed another pot of coffee, and then sat down and made a list of the things he was going to have to buy in town. Then he built up the fire in the fireplace and fixed a cup of coffee. Sitting on the edge of the bunk, he rolled himself a smoke.

"I'm going to have to buy a chair," he said. "Maybe a rocking chair," he mused. "Hell, why not just go ahead and file on this place? It's quiet enough. There hasn't been one person ride by since I got here, and this strike probably won't last long. It'll be a place to come back to. Yeah, I'll do that. That suit you, Dog?"

Dog wagged his tail.

"All right. That's settled."

Frank had money. Vivian had left him a percentage of the Henson Company and Conrad had not contested it. Frank didn't know how much it was worth, but knew it was considerable. He probably would never have to worry about money again.

He smiled at that thought, thinking: *Hell, I've never worried about money in my life.* He got up to pour another cup of coffee, and was walking back to the bunk when he heard a wagon rattle up and the driver whoa his team.

Frank told Dog to stay put and to his surprise, the animal obeyed him. He stepped outside on the small porch.

"Howdy," the man on the wagon seat called.

"Howdy," Frank replied.

"You settlin' in, hey?" Before Frank could reply, the man said, "Well, you can shore have it, mister. That damn Henson Company's done got all the good claims sewed up tighter than a miser's purse."

"I'll just look around and maybe try my hand at panning."

"Good luck to you."

"Thanks. Say, you don't know who owns this place, do you?"

"Nobody, mister. Same with my place down the way. I done checked on that. Too far away from the strike. You wouldn't be interested in buyin' some furniture, would you? I'd sure like to lighten this load."

"Maybe. What do you have?"

Frank bought a table and chairs, a rocking chair, a bed with a nice feather tick, some bedding, a washtub, and some dishes and cooking utensils. It was too late to ride into the nearest land office to check on the property; he would do that tomorrow.

Frank arranged his new purchases, and found that he had suddenly turned a cabin into a home. Dog carefully smelled each new piece of furniture, and then walked over to his place under the bunk, lay down, and went to sleep.

It was full dark outside and a cold wind was blowing. Frank built a fire, made sure there was water in Dog's bucket, then went to bed.

He went to sleep with a smile on his face.

He liked this quiet place. Maybe he had found a home after all his long years of wandering.

He hoped so.

Four

Frank put Dog's bedding on the front porch and told the animal to stay. The dog lay down and looked at him.

"I'll be back," Frank told him. "Count on it. And if I decide to leave for good, you'll go with me. All right?"

Dog yawned.

"I'll take that as a yes." Frank mounted up and rode into the mining camp.

The new town, as yet unnamed, was crowded with men seeking their fortune. A few wore pistols; most did not. Frank did not see anyone who looked or dressed like a gunfighter or trouble-hunter. But they would come, he was sure of that.

He went to the same general store he'd stopped at the day before, and bought enough supplies to last him for a week or so. Then he walked over to the land office and filed on his land.

"You sure filed on a lot of land. You find something way out there, mister?" the clerk asked.

"No, and I'm not looking. It's quiet out there and that's the way I like it."

The clerk looked down at the name, then

blinked and looked again. "Are you really?..."
He swallowed hard and met Frank's eyes.

"Yes, I am."

"Well, ah...I mean. Ah...welcome to Gold Camp, Mr. Morgan."

"Gold Camp?"

"That what some folks has taken to calling this place."

"It's as good as any name, I suppose." Frank looked at the papers he'd just signed. "Is that it?"

"That's it, Mr. Morgan. You now own, if you prove it up and keep the taxes paid, one hundred and sixty acres of the most worthless land in this territory."

Frank smiled. "It's priceless to me."

"You plannin' on doin' some pannin'?"

"No. I just want to live quietly."

"Good luck."

Frank left the land office and walked over to the nearest cafe. He had an early lunch, which wasn't very good, then decided to walk around the fast-growing town and get a feel for his surroundings.

He hadn't walked fifty yards before he spotted Conrad Browning walking up the newly laid and rough boardwalk on the other side of the street. Frank quickly stepped into a saloon and stood on one side of the batwings, watching his son.

Conrad had two men with him, one in front, one in the rear. Bodyguards obviously. Very capable-looking men, but judging by their dress, not Western men.

Conrad walked on up the street and out of sight. Frank sighed and turned around, walking to the long bar. He really didn't want a drink, but to better fit in with the already crowded bar, he ordered a beer.

Outside, the sounds of hammering and sawing easily penetrated the canvas-covered wooden frame of the saloon. Many of the buildings in the mining camp were canvas and wood. They would last just about as long as the gold strike, Frank figured. Maybe through the winter.

Frank sipped his beer, which was flat-tasting, and listened to the talk all around him. So far, no one had recognized him and pointed him out, but that was just a matter of time, for the man at the land office would be sure to spread the word.

Sipping his beer, Frank thought about making this his permanent home. If he was going to do that, and he was determined to do it, he'd better get busy building a small barn, or adding on to the lean-to, installing windows in the cabin, and building a fence around it.

Frank set his beer mug down on the bar. He'd start with that right now.

Back on the street, Frank stopped to ask questions of a crew working on a permanent structure on the main street.

"Where did you boys get the lumber and nails and such?" Frank asked.

One of the men pointed up the long and busy street. "See that fellow yonder in the lead freight wagon, just stopping in front of the

31

Lucky Lode Saloon? That's Wally Spalding. He runs a sawmill and freight service. He'll fix you right up, for a price, and he ain't cheap."

"Thanks."

Frank arranged with Wally for several loads of lumber to be delivered to his cabin. Wally said he had it in stock and would deliver it to his place the next day, along with nails and such. Frank started to pay the man on the spot, and Wally smiled and held up a hand.

"I know who are you, Morgan. I recognized you right off. Your word is good with me. You're going to need a hammer and saw and file and everything else, I reckon. I'll bring it and you can pick it out."

Frank thanked the man and said he'd see him the next day. Then he walked over to the general store and did some more shopping. His packhorse was loaded down with supplies when he rode out of town.

Dog was so excited to see Frank, he almost spooked the horses with his barking and racing around the yard when Frank rode up to the side of the cabin.

Frank calmed him down and got the horses in the lean-to, then began carrying his supplies into the cabin and putting them away.

"Shelves," he said aloud. "Have to build some shelves too." He looked around the cabin. "And have some lady in town fix up curtains for me." He smiled. "After I replace the glass, that is."

Frank built a fire in the cookstove, fixed a

pot of coffee, had a couple of cups and a smoke, then started toting in water to heat. He carefully scrubbed and washed all the bedding he'd bought from the mover, and hung it out to dry, although as cool as it was, the bedding would probably take twenty-four hours to dry. Then he heated more water and washed all the dishes he'd bought.

"Damn, a lot of housework," Frank muttered, sitting down to have another cup of coffee. He pulled off his boots and found his moccasins. "Who says women don't work around the home?" Before he pulled on the soft moccasins, he noticed his big toe sticking out of a hole in his sock. "Something else to repair," he said. Then he remembered that he didn't have any needles or thread. "Or throw them away and buy new ones," he decided aloud.

That reminded him that he'd better write a letter to his lawyers and see how much money he had earned from his shares in the Henson Company, and how much he had left. He'd do that right now, and ride into the mining camp after his lumber was delivered and post the letter.

Then he remembered he had no paper or pen or ink. "Damn!" he said. "Something else to buy."

Dog left his place under the bunk and came to Frank's side by the chair. Frank petted the animal. "Lots of things to do, boy," he said. "But what the hell? I've got nothing but time."

Frank stood up and took off his shirt, removing the money belt he wore around his waist. He knew he had ample funds. But the belt was uncomfortable, chafing him. He spent the next hour carefully digging out a rock on the outside far left side of the fireplace, close to the floor. He hid much of his money there and replaced the rock. The cabin could burn down and his money would be safe...he hoped.

There was no bank as yet in the town called Gold Camp. But Frank knew if the town lasted for any length of time, someone like Wells Fargo would come in with some kind of banking institution or repository.

The shadows were deepening around the cabin when Frank finally called it quits for the day and started thinking about supper for himself and Dog.

He put some beans on, sliced bacon, and made ready to fix some pan bread. Then he lit the lamps and filled the cabin with welcome light. While supper was cooking, Frank found the book he'd bought in town from a peddler and read for a time. It was a small book of poetry by Robert Browning.

Frank read:

I give the fight up: let there be an end.
A privacy, an obscure nook for me.
I want to be forgotten even by God.

Frank closed the volume and sat for a time. "Yes," he finally said, as he rose from the chair, walking to the stove to turn the thick-sliced bacon. "That's me. I give up the fight. The Pine and Vanbergen gangs can go their own way as long as they leave me alone." He had known all along that Vivian would not want him to risk his life for her memory.

And if Conrad is touched by all this? The thought jumped into his brain.

He's a grown man running a multi-million-dollar company, Frank thought. He can afford to hire an army to fight his battles. Besides, he doesn't want anything to do with me. He made that clear enough several months ago.

No, he's got to learn to stand on his own. Especially if he wants to make it out here in the West. Folks out here still demand that a man saddle his own horse and stomp on his own snakes.

He stirred the beans and added some sliced onions to flavor up the beans. Supper wouldn't be long now.

Dog padded over and sat by the stove, looking up at him. "Won't be long, boy," Frank told him. "It ain't much but I'm sure gonna share. Fifty-fifty, Dog. Gotta put some weight on you. You're plumb skinny. I figure another ten pounds and you'll be about right."

That would put the animal at about forty pounds.

Frank and Dog ate supper, and Frank put Dog outside to do his business. It had turned much colder and Frank built a fire in the fireplace, letting the fire in the stove slowly die out. There would be a blanket of frost on the ground come morning. Wasn't long before Dog scratched at the door and Frank let him in. Dog went immediately to his bed, curled up, and went to sleep.

"I won't be far behind you, boy."

Frank checked on the horses, did a quick walk-around of his place, and then turned in. Tomorrow was going to be a busy day for sure.

Frank slept deep and dreamless, rising about four o'clock. And it was sure enough cold. He quick-stepped to the privy and back, shivering both ways. He made coffee and fixed some bacon and bread, then sat in front of the fireplace until the chill left his bones.

Spalding's freight wagons were at Frank's place by nine o'clock, the men off-loading his building materials, including hammers and nails, several saws and axes, one of them a broadaxe and another a hand adz.

"Mr. Spalding said you can catch him in his office in town sometime and pay him off, Mr. Morgan. We'll see you. Take it easy and don't work too hard now."

Frank looked at the huge pile of lumber by the side of the house as the empty freight wagons rattled off down the road. "Of course not," he muttered.

Frank was no expert carpenter, but he knew the fundamentals of building. He went to work.

Frank worked sunup to sundown for the next several weeks, riding into town only twice during that period, once to arrange for a load of hay to be delivered. He built a small barn for the horses, adding it on to the lean-to. He added a room to the cabin and then built a fence around the cabin, taking in about an acre. The glass for the windows arrived and Frank installed that. His carpentry work was not expert by any means, but it was functional. Frank had recalled and kept in mind what a workman had told him years back, "Measure twice and cut once."

On his second trip into town, Frank picked up a letter posted to him by attorneys representing the Henson Company. Frank sat for a long time digesting the contents of the letter detailing just how much money he had earned from his stock in the company. It was difficult for him to accept, for it was a staggering amount.

Frank was a moderately rich man for the times. He would never again have to worry about money.

With ninety percent of the work done, Frank decided to take a day off and ride into town for supplies. He was running out of essentials.

When he returned late that afternoon, his cabin had been burned to the ground and Dog was lying still in the front yard. He had been shot. There was a note nailed to the gate.

MORGAN: WE BURNED YOUR
SHACK AND KILLED YOUR
DAMN STUPID DOG. ITS YOUR

MOVE. COME GET US YOU SON
OF A BITCH.

It was signed Ned Pine and Vic Vanbergen.

Five

Passing by the still form of Dog, Frank saw one of the animal's back legs twitch. Dog was still alive. Frank knelt down and inspected his pet. There was a wound on Dog's side, and the top of his head was bloody. Frank got his canteen, wet a bandanna, and cleaned the head wound. A bullet had creased Dog's head, leaving a gash, and knocking the animal unconscious, but Frank did not think it was serious. Then he looked at the wound in Dog's side. A bullet must have ricocheted off something, tearing the lead apart. A small piece of lead was imbedded in Dog's side. Frank popped it out with the point of his knife. He picked Dog up and carried him back to the lean-to, placing him on a pile of hay. Dog would either come out of his stupor, or he would not. There was nothing else Frank could do.

Frank looked at the still-smoking and hot embers that were once his cabin. He had lost everything.

He walked over to the fireplace, thinking he would dig out his money from the fireplace stones, but it was still too hot. The log cabin would have burned quickly, so Frank figured the fire had been set no more than a couple of hours ago. Maybe less than that. It would probably be another hour before he could dig out his money.

He walked back to check on Dog. The animal was still breathing but still unconscious.

Frank unloaded his supplies, stashing them in the new addition to the lean-to, then stabled his horses. He could spend the night in the small new addition. It would be cold, but he had experienced worse in his time. He got a shovel and dug a hole in the ground, in the center of the barn, lining the outside area of the hole with rocks, then built a small fire. It would knock the chill off and keep a man warm, if he stayed close enough to the fire.

He heard Dog whimper, and knelt down beside the animal. "Well, ol' boy," he said. "Glad to see you alive. You just lay still for a time and you'll be all right."

Dog licked his hand and Frank carefully petted him. "You want some water, boy. I'll get you some."

Frank found Dog's outside bowl and filled it with water. Dog drank half the bowl's contents, then laid his head back down on the hay and closed his eyes.

"Rest is good for you, Dog. I know. I been shot a few times myself."

Frank found the small coffeepot he used on the trail and started water boiling. He had eaten a good meal in town and wasn't hungry. But he was getting mad.

He sat for a time, letting hot anger wash over him. Frank drank a cup of good strong coffee and glanced over at Dog. The animal was awake and looking at him. Dog wagged his tail, and Frank smiled at him. "I been told that more men have died fighting over God and animals than have been killed fighting over women. I believe it. They shouldn't have shot you, fellow. I can rebuild a cabin. But you...that's another story."

Frank leaned back against a support post and sipped his coffee. He thought: *I was going to live and let live, boys. The hunt was going to end right here. But you boys don't want that. All right. Suits me. But you better bear one thing in mind: You started this dance. Now, by God, you'd better be ready to pay the band.*

Frank dozed lightly through the night, awakening often to check on Dog and to build up the small fire. Come daylight, Dog was standing up on his own. He was a bit shaky, and hobbled around with a limp, but he was going to make it.

Frank dug out the stones around the base of the fireplace and retrieved his money. Some of the bills were a bit crispy around the edges, but spendable.

Frank found a skillet in the rubble and cleaned it up. Then he sliced some bacon and started it frying. Frank and Dog had bacon and pan bread for breakfast.

After some food, Frank checked Dog's wounds and cleaned them, applying some antiseptic...which Dog did not like at all,

40

showing his teeth in protest. But he made no attempt to bite Frank.

Frank lounged around the ruins of his cabin for several days. When he was sure Dog was well on the way to healing, Frank packed up. He fixed Dog a place to ride on one side of the packsaddle, and on a very cold and frosty morning, pulled out. He headed first into the mining camp and bought supplies and new clothing. Then he had a bath and shave and haircut.

"You ready to hit the trail, boy?" he asked Dog, resting in his perch on the packsaddle.

Dog barked.

"Let's do it then."

In the saddle, Frank glanced across the street. His son, Conrad, was standing in front of a tent cafe, looking at him. Frank smiled and lifted a hand in greeting. His son nodded his head curtly and without expression, then turned and walked away, his bodyguards with him.

The coldness of the young man neither surprised nor upset Frank. Conrad did not like his father and had never made any attempt to hide his feelings. Frank lifted the reins and rode on out of the mining camp. He did not look back.

Frank also had a hunch that Conrad would haul his ashes out for a warmer clime before icy winter locked up everything.

Frank had received word on the way to Denver that the Pine and Vanbergen gangs would not winter in the deep Rockies. It was just too damn cold and the gangs ran the risk of getting snowed in and trapped. Frank did not know whether to believe that or not, but without a warm place to hole up, he had no desire to stay in the middle of the high country when the temperature dropped to thirty below zero.

Frank headed southwest. He had him a hunch, and he often played out his hunches. Besides, Frank had learned that the southwest part of Colorado Territory was Pine's old stomping grounds. He had kin down there. Ned had not been born there, but came to that part of the territory when he was run out of wherever the hell he did come from...and the stories about that were many and varied. The stories about Vic were also many and varied. No one really knew what to believe about either of the gang leaders, except that they were both vicious killers without a shred of morals or conscience.

The area around Durango had more than its share of gold and silver mines that were still producing, there was lots of money floating around, and that would be a good place for the gangs to winter. Although Frank knew that the winters down there could be tough.

Frank was in no hurry, and he stopped often to check his back trail and to let Dog limp around, stretch his legs, and tend to business. Dog was healing fast and putting on weight, each day spending more time on the ground and less time riding the pack animal.

Frank was astonished at the number of

people he saw on his way south. The country was filling up fast and settling.

Indian trouble was, for the most part, over. There would occasionally be a band of young bucks jumping the reservation and causing some trouble, but that was happening less and less as more settlers moved in.

Frank spent a lot of time wondering why Pine and Vanbergen would do such a stupid thing as hunt him down and burn him out, then leave a direct challenge for him to come get them.

"Arrogance, I reckon," Frank muttered. He had been on the trail for a week, and had just entered the high grassland basin in the center of Colorado Territory, on the east side of the Platte. He had made camp for the evening with a lot of daylight left and had just dumped in the coffee and pulled the pot off the fire, setting it on the rocks that circled the small fire. He added a bit of cold water to settle the grounds, and leaned back against his saddle. Dog was lying by him when the animal suddenly raised his head and uttered a low growl.

"Easy," Frank said, putting a hand on Dog's head. "Quiet now, boy."

"Hello, the fire." The shout came out of the brush. "I'm friendly. That coffee sure smells good."

"Come on in," Frank called. His hand was on the butt of his .45.

A young man stepped into the small clearing, leading his horse. The man looked to be in his mid-twenties and was not wearing a pistol...at least none that Frank could see.

"Howdy," the young man said. "Name is Jeff Barton."

"Glad to meet you," Frank said. "I'm Frank. Come on in. Coffee will be ready in a few minutes."

"Let me take care of my horse," Jeff said. "He's tired."

"Looks it. There's a little crick over there." Frank pointed. "Come a long way?"

"A fair distance," Jeff replied. He let his horse drink a little, then pulled him back, stripped the saddle from him, and hobbled the animal. He got a cup from his saddlebags and walked over to the fire, settling down with a sigh of contentment.

Frank hid his knowing smile. Jeff was no horseman. He was butt-sore. "Weary some?"

"You bet. It's that obvious, hey?"

"Somewhat. New to this country?"

"New to the West," Jeff admitted with a smile. "Tell you the truth, Frank, I'm sort of lost."

Frank chuckled. "Heading for the goldfields?"

"Yes. You?"

"I'm going that way. But I'm no miner. Doesn't interest me."

Jeff looked at him. "Gold doesn't interest you?"

"Not unless I can find it laying on top of the ground, within easy reach. I guess the gold bug never bit me. Where did you get your horse?"

"My horse? Oh...in Denver. Something wrong with him?"

"It isn't a him, it's a mare. Where are you from?"

"New York City. I, ah, don't know much about horses. But I did know it was a mare. I guess I'm what you Westerners call a tenderfoot."

Dog walked over and smelled the newcomer, then backed away and lay back down beside Frank.

"Do I pass inspection?" Jeff asked.

"He didn't bite you."

"I see. Why did you ask about my horse?"

"She's a very tired animal. Needs a day or two of rest. That's an awful lot of stuff you had hanging off of her."

"Oh. Well... I'll just do that then."

"Need to get you a packhorse."

"I wonder why the livery man in Denver didn't tell me that."

"Did you ask about one?"

"Ah...no."

"Have some coffee. It'll cheer you up. You hungry?"

"Come to think of it, I am."

"I'm going to have bacon and beans and pan bread. How's that sound?"

"Sounds very good. I'm not much of a cook."

Or much of a horseman, Frank thought, eyeballing the piece-of-crap saddle Jeff had stripped from his horse. *Somebody saw you coming, boy.*

Frank put the beans on to cook and settled back with his cup of coffee. "You know anything about mining, Jeff?"

45

"I read some books on the subject."

"Well, that's a start, I reckon."

"I really wanted to get out of New York and start over here in the West."

"You're not wanted by the law, are you?" Frank asked with a smile.

"Oh, no!" Jeff said quickly, then realized that Frank was kidding him. "My fiancée decided she didn't want me either."

"Ahh, I see. Affairs of the heart. I can certainly understand that."

"I was devastated."

"Drink your coffee, you'll feel better."

"It's amazing, really. But in the weeks I've been gone, her face is becoming dimmer in my mind."

Then it wasn't love, boy, Frank thought. *Vivian's face is as fresh in my mind now as it was twenty years ago.*

"If you don't mind me saying so, Frank, you look familiar to me. I could swear I've seen you somewhere. Have you ever been to New York?"

"Never have, Jeff."

"You certainly remind me of someone." Jeff stared at Frank for a moment, then softly exclaimed, "Oh, my God!"

"What's wrong?"

"You're Frank Morgan!"

"That's my name, boy."

"I saw a likeness of you on the cover of a book I read. You're the gunfighter!"

"I been called that, Jeff."

"You've killed five hundred white men and

a thousand Indians! Good Lord! I'm actually sitting here conversing with the most famous gunfighter in all the West."

Frank chuckled as he poured another cup of coffee. "Those figures are a tad high, Jeff. Don't believe everything you read in those dime novels."

"I thought you would be a lot older, Mr. Morgan."

"I do sometimes feel a lot older, for a fact."

"I did not mean that as a slur, sir."

"I know it. And stop calling me sir. My name is Frank. How's your coffee?"

"What? Oh. It's delicious."

"Want another cup?"

"Yes, please. I'm afraid I haven't discovered the knack of making good coffee on the trail."

"Boil the water and dump it in. Then add some cold water to settle the grounds."

"I'll remember that. What is your dog's name, sir...ah, Frank?"

"Dog."

"Well...that certainly fits him."

Frank laughed at that. He liked this young tenderfoot, and wondered how he'd gotten this far without running smack into danger. "Tell you what, Jeff. You can tag along with me. I'm heading down your way."

"You mean that?"

"I said it."

"That would be grand!"

"All right, then. Let's have another cup of coffee and I'll show you how to make pan bread."

47

"I'm very grateful to you, sir...ah, Frank. That means a lot to me."

Dog raised his head and growled, looking off toward the north. Frank's .45 appeared in his hand, hammer back. Jeff sat staring, his eyes bugged out.

"My word!" the young man said. "I didn't even see you pull the gun out."

"Comes with practice. Now be quiet."

Dog growled again, low in his throat, his ears laid back, teeth bared.

"Steady, boy," Frank whispered. "Let them come on."

"Who is it, do you suppose?" Jeff whispered.

"Someone up to no good, you can bet on that."

Frank heard the faint metallic click of a hammer being jacked back, and shoved Jeff backward. "Stay down!" he said, then threw himself to one side just as the late afternoon air was filled with gunsmoke and lead.

Six

Frank's .45 roared five times, so fast Jeff could not count them. Frank rolled to one side, grabbed his .44-40, and cut loose with it.

Dog ran behind Frank's saddle and stayed there.

One of the bullets from the hidden ambushers

hit the coffeepot and blew a hole in it, knocking the pot spinning. Another punctured the small pot of beans and knocked it off one side of the rocks and into the fire.

"There goes supper," Frank muttered. "Damnit!"

"Get 'im!" the shout came from behind the brush.

A man burst out of the brush just to Frank's right, and Frank spun around and drilled him in the brisket. The .44-40 round doubled the man over and sat him down on his butt.

"Oh, God!" the gut-shot man yelled.

"Stupid play," Frank said, levering another round into his rifle. He waited.

"Cloy?" The one-word question was thrown out from somewhere to Frank's left.

Whoever Cloy was, he either couldn't or didn't reply.

One of my bullets must have hit him, Frank thought. *Lucky shot.*

"Daniel?" the voice called.

"I've had it, Jack. Hard-hit in the belly." Then Daniel started yelling as the pain struck him, hot and heavy.

"To hell with the kid and to hell with you," Jack said. "I'm gone outta here."

"You can't just leave me!" Daniel hollered.

"Watch me," Jack said.

Frank emptied his rifle where he thought the hidden voice was coming from, and quickly reloaded.

"What kid are they talking about?" Jeff asked.

"You, I reckon. They must have thought you had some money."

"I wish."

"I'm a-hurtin' somethang fierce," Daniel hollered. "Y'all got to hep me!"

"Go to hell," Frank told him.

"You cain't mean that! We didn't mean you a bit of harm, mister. We was after the kid's money, that's all. Oh, God, I hurt so bad."

"Tough luck," Frank told him.

"Jack!" Daniel hollered. "Oh, Jack."

Jack did not respond.

Frank waited.

"Help me, Jack!" Daniel yelled, his voice much weaker.

A faint groan came from the brush. Then a thrashing sound. Then silence.

"I think Jack is beyond help, Daniel," Frank called.

Daniel cursed him. "You'll rot in hell for this," he said. "We didn't mean you no hurt. There wasn't no need for you to shoot us."

"You're a fool."

"Now what?" Jeff asked.

"We wait," Frank told him. "Stay down."

"Are you going to help those wounded men?"

"Hell, no."

Several minutes passed in silence. There was no more sound from the brush and Daniel's moaning ceased.

"Stay put," Frank told the young man.

"What are you going to do?"

"Check it out. Don't move and keep your head down."

Frank eased out of cover and slipped into the brush. He had taken only a few steps before he found Jack's body. One of his .44-40 rounds had struck the man in the center of his chest. He moved on and found the body of the man called Cloy. He had taken a round from Frank's pistol in the center of his forehead. Frank walked back to the clearing and looked down at Daniel. The gut-shot man stared back at him through pain-filled eyes.

"My pals?" Daniel asked.

"Dead."

"You an evil man, you are."

"And you're a fool."

"What be your name? I got a right to know that much, don't you think?"

"Frank Morgan."

"Oh, good God!" Daniel said. He sighed and shook his head. "Frank Morgan!"

"You got any kin that might give a damn about your dying?" Frank asked.

"I got a brother and sister up in Oregon. But they disowned me years ago."

"I don't blame them. Anybody else?"

Jeff walked up, his face pale. Dog had wisely elected to stay behind cover.

Daniel cut his eyes to the young man. He took a deep breath and shuddered in pain. "I hate you."

"Why?" Jeff questioned. "What did I ever do to you?"

Daniel shifted his gaze back to Frank. "And I hate you too, Morgan."

"I'm overcome with grief."

Daniel closed his eyes and never opened them again.

"Is he dead?" Jeff asked.

"Yep."

"The others?"

"Stone dead."

"They were going to kill me for the few dollars I have, weren't they?"

"Yep. They sure were."

"Now what?"

"Have you ever fired a pistol?" Frank asked.

"No."

"Rifle?"

"No. But I fired a shotgun once."

"Wonderful. Get the pistol belts from the dead. I'll get their horses."

"You want me to handle the dead?"

"Do you know of a better way to remove their gunbelts, Jeff?"

"Ah...no, I guess not."

"They won't bother you."

"I suppose not. Very well."

Frank found the horses about a hundred yards from the clearing. They were all fine animals. Frank wondered if they were stolen. He led them back to the creek and let them drink, then stripped the saddles and bridles from them, then went through the bedrolls and saddlebags.

He found a coffeepot and a cook pot and laid them aside. He found a bill of sale for the chestnut and read it. It looked legitimate enough. Frank could transfer sale to Jeff easily enough.

"What are you going to do with the dead people?" Jeff asked.

"Kick some dirt over them and then start supper."

Jeff swallowed hard and then cleared his throat. "You're certainly taking this calmly."

"No point in getting all excited about it. It's over."

"I owe you my life, Frank."

Frank shrugged that off. "Life is still pretty cheap out here. Not as cheap as it was ten years ago, but many folks are still fairly casual about killings."

"I'm beginning to understand that. There was a shooting during a train stop in Kansas. Two men shot it out in the middle of the street."

"Who won?"

"They both were shot."

"Happens that way more often than not. Come on. Let's get the dead buried and then see about supper."

"I'm afraid I've lost my appetite, Frank."

"You'll get it back."

The gunfighter and the tenderfoot drifted southwest. They were in no hurry and stopped often. Dog spent more and more time on the ground now, only occasionally riding along in the pouch on the packsaddle.

The ambushers had had about a hundred dollars between them, and Frank gave that to Jeff, along with a new bill of sale for the horse.

53

"Those old boys won't be needing them, Jeff. First town we come to, I'll sell the other horses and you can have that money. Be a good grubstake for you."

"Grubstake," Jeff said. "What an interesting word."

Once, just once, Frank gave Jeff a lesson in the art of pistol shooting. He backed off about ten paces from a huge old stump, carefully handed Jeff the pistol, and told him to hit it.

Jeff hit everything but the stump.

"I think you better concentrate on learning how to use a rifle, Jeff. You don't need to be wearing a pistol. Out here, somebody is liable to call your hand and make you use it."

"I think you're right."

Jeff turned out to be a pretty fair hand with a rifle. After a week of daily practice he could usually hit what he was aiming at.

At a small-town livery, Frank sold the spare horses and gave Jeff the money. "Hang onto that. We'll sell the guns at the next town."

"I'm going to have a nice reserve of cash."

"You'll need it in these gold camps. Things tend to be a mite expensive."

"I'm going to hate to part company, Frank. This has been quite a learning experience for me."

"Oh, I'll be around, Jeff. Besides, we've got a ways to go yet."

"I was hoping I'd get to see some wild Indians."

Frank smiled. "Not many of those still active, Jeff. But believe me, you really don't want to run into any Injuns on the warpath."

54

"But you have, right?"

"A time or two."

"Did you fight them?"

"When I had to. I avoided a fight whenever I could."

"You did?"

"Damn right. Injuns were mean fighters. Once they got their dander up, they wouldn't cut a man any slack."

"Where did all the Indians go?"

"On reservations mostly. Those that weren't killed or died from disease or starvation. We're in Ute country now. But it's doubtful we'll see any. They're mostly on reservations down in the southwest corner of the territory."

"Doesn't seem fair to me. It was their land, wasn't it?"

"It wasn't anybody's land, Jeff."

"What do you mean?"

"What happened to the Injuns that lived back East when the pilgrims arrived a couple of hundred years ago?"

"Why...I guess I don't know."

"Shoved out of the way, moved west, killed off, died from disease, that's what. Same thing out here. Easterners, some of them, tend to look down their noses at the way the Injuns were, and are, treated out here. But they were done the same way back East, for the most part."

"I guess they were, at that. But the West is so, well, violent."

"Blown all out of proportion, Jeff. Because

Easterners have a short memory. The West is a new land, just like the East was two hundred years ago. Those early settlers in America fought for their right to be here and make something of this land."

"You're an educated man, Frank. You've done a lot of thinking about a lot of subjects."

"Self-taught, Jeff. I got through part of grade school as a kid, that's all."

"But you could have been whatever you wanted to be. I know that. You're a very intelligent man. I've noticed those books you carry around with you."

"But I settled on being a gunfighter?" Frank said, amusement in his voice.

"Well...I really didn't mean it like that."

"I'm just kidding you, Jeff."

"Oh...all right. Frank?"

"Yep."

"We're running a little low on supplies."

"Yeah. We're about a day and a half out of Salida. We'll provision up close to there at a little place I know near some springs. Salida used to be called South Arkansas; then some folks renamed it. The whole damn area is tough, so stay close and watch your mouth."

"Don't you worry about that. I am your silent partner."

"Still lots of hanging in that area, especially in Buena Vista. That's a mean judge there. I came through there about five years ago and counted five bodies swinging out on the edge of town."

"Surely you're joking."

"Nope. His name is Judge Lynch."

"Now I know you're kidding me!"

"Nope. I sure am not. That's his name. Quite a number of whorehouses in those towns. One-Eyed Sally's got the biggest one."

"You've been in them?"

"Nope. But I've ridden past them a few times. They do quite a business, let me tell you."

"Judge Lynch?"

Frank laughed at his young friend. "That's right. But we'll cut south of that town."

"Oh?"

"Yep. I know a shortcut over to Buffalo Pass and then we'll follow the Saguache for a ways down to a stage stop and tradin' post. After that it really gets into some wild country. You'll see the beauty of the territory. Something you'll remember for the rest of your life."

"Wilder than this?"

"Son, you haven't seen nothin' yet."

Seven

"I've lost all sense of time out here," Jeff said. "What is the date?"

"I think it's November," Frank replied. "But I wouldn't take any bets on it."

"My word! It'll be Christmas before long."

"I reckon so."

"You celebrate Christmas, don't you?"

"Not in a long time, Jeff."

"I always enjoyed the holidays. It's such a wonderful gay time."

"You have family back there?"

"Oh, yes. My parents. My brothers and sisters. Uncles and aunts and lots of cousins."

"Think you'll go back someday?"

Jeff didn't immediately reply and Frank understood: The West could cast a powerful spell on a man. It could be pure hell on a woman, but many men who traveled out here ended up staying. The vastness of the West could be hypnotic.

"I don't know, Frank," Jeff finally replied. "If I can make some kind of living out here, I believe I'll stay."

"I thought that might be your answer. Doesn't take long for the West to grab hold on a man."

Jeff looked up at the sky. "Looks odd."

"Looks like snow," Frank told him. "And it might be a heavy one too. Or it might blow past. Anyway, we're only a few miles from the Springs. We'll hole up there until it blows over. Give the horses some rest and we'll provision up. Maybe get us a bath."

"I itch all over," Jeff said.

"Cooties."

"Sounds disgusting. And my clothes are filthy."

"Welcome to the trail, Jeff. It isn't so bad during the spring and summer. Man with a bar of soap can get himself a good wash in a creek or river. It gets tough during the cold months. We'll get our clothes washed there too. Then the hard pull starts."

"How far are we from Durango?"

"Couple of weeks."

"The vastness of the West is very nearly overwhelming. For a couple of days after leaving Denver I saw people. Then...nothing."

"Lots of time for a man to think."

"Introspection."

"I reckon."

The trading post that Frank had mentioned was gone. It had burned down and not been rebuilt.

"Well, I'll just be damned," Frank said, looking at the old ashes.

"Now what?"

"I reckon we ride into town after all."

"Buena Vista?"

"No. Salida's closer. 'Bout five miles east of here. Down that road there. And it's a tad calmer. They got a hotel too. We'll get us a couple of rooms and sleep in a real bed."

"After we bathe, I hope," Jeff said dryly.

It was midafternoon when the pair rode into town. Just before the ride in, Frank had put Dog in the pouch on the packsaddle and told him to stay put. He took Dog into the hotel with him. The desk clerk at the hotel got real huffy about Dog staying in Frank's room...until Frank signed the register, and the clerk stared at his name for a moment, swallowing hard a couple of times. When the desk clerk could finally speak, he allowed as to how it would be just fine for Dog to stay in Frank's room.

"You go on up to the rooms and take Dog with you," Frank told Jeff. "I've got to do a little banking. It won't take long. Then we'll get us a bath and new duds."

"Ah, Frank...I think I'd better save my money."

"Relax. I have plenty of money. My treat."

"Are you sure? I don't know when I'll be able to repay you."

"Don't worry about it, Jeff. I assure you, I have ample funds."

At the bank, Frank asked to speak to the manager and was shown into his office. There, Frank opened a canvas and oilskin pouch and took out one of several bank drafts he carried with him. "Cash this for me?" he asked the manager.

"This is for a lot of money, sir. Are you sure you want to carry this much cash with you?"

"I'm sure."

"We'll be happy to honor this draft, of course." He again looked at the name. "Ah...are you really..." He pointed to the name on the bank draft.

"I am," Frank said. "In the flesh. You have a problem with that?"

"Oh, no, sir! Not at all. I shall be right back with your money."

"Told you it wouldn't take long," Frank said, walking into the adjoining hotel rooms. "You ready for a bath and some new duds?"

"I am."

"Bring Dog."

"Is he going to get a bath too?"

"He sure is."

Frank bought them both new clothes at a general store; then they walked over to a barbershop that also advertised hot baths. After Frank finished washing off days of dirt, he dunked Dog several times in the hot soapy water. They both smelled better, although Dog didn't seem to appreciate his bath nearly as much as Frank did.

All decked out in new clothes and feeling much better, Frank stashed Dog in the hotel room with a big bowl of stew he'd ordered from the dining room and a washbasin full of water. Then he and Jeff went down to the hotel's dining room for supper.

The desk clerk and the bank employees had spread the word about Frank Morgan being in town, and a crowd had gathered in the hotel lobby, including the marshal and all his deputies.

"You create more of a stir than the mayor of New York City," Jeff remarked.

"Which is why I try to avoid towns as much as possible. Ignore the people. Let's get something to eat."

After a few minutes of nothing happening, much of the crowd began to drift away, but the marshal and one of his deputies stayed, seated at a table away from Frank and Jeff, drinking coffee and staying ready for trouble.

Frank and his new partner ate a tough steak and some undercooked potatoes and overcooked bread, and left the dining room, retiring to their rooms.

"They should have given us that meal free, just for eating it," Jeff said. "That was awful."

"Sure wasn't anything to write home about," Frank agreed. "Good night, Jeff. See you in the morning."

"Are we pulling out then?"

"If we're not stuck here by heavy snow. If so, we'll wait it out."

Frank took Dog outside to do his business, taking the steps down the back way to avoid any gawkers that might still be in the hotel lobby. The night air was cold but the skies were clear and starry. The clouds had drifted on.

"We might get out of here tomorrow, Dog," Frank whispered. "I hope."

Back in his room, Frank built a small fire in the stove, wedged a straight-backed chair under the doorknob, and went to bed. He was up and moving at five in the morning. He took Dog out for a walk in the alley and found the ground snow-free. It was cold, but far from being unbearably so. Frank rolled Jeff out of bed.

"Let's get the hell out of this town, Jeff."

"Suits me. We going across the mountains?"

"Maybe. Depends on the weather. We'll know in a day or two. Then we'll decide."

The men were riding out of the town an hour later, Dog resting in his pouch on the packsaddle.

Frank cut south after checking the sky several times. It was flat-looking, had a strangeness to it that Frank didn't like.

"I figure we can make it over the pass in a few hours," Frank said. "Then we'll pick up the road through the valley. Beats the hell out of being caught in the mountains during a blizzard."

"How far is the nearest town?"

"Day and a half. Maybe two days of easy riding. But there is a stage stop halfway. I know it's still there 'cause the stage is still running. We can make that easy."

They made the stage stop by early evening, and got their horses stabled just as the sky began dumping snow: great big wet flakes that clung to a person's clothing for a few seconds before melting. The stage had arrived and was going to be there for a while, maybe all night. A busted axle. The passengers, four men and two women, were just sitting down to supper when Frank and Jeff walked in.

"Howdy, boys," the stationmaster called. "Come on in. Got beans and beef and biscuits for supper."

"Sounds good," Frank said. "Got any coffee ready?"

" 'Bout a gallon over yonder." He jerked his head. "Help yourself."

The stage driver came in rubbing his hands. "Three more men comin' in," he told the stationmaster. "Better toss some more steaks in the skillet and give the beans another stir. And it's snowin' so hard you can't hardly see your hand in front of your face."

Frank had poured himself a cup of coffee and stepped back into the deep shadows of the big room. He had fixed Dog a place in the stable with the horses, and fed him with chunks of the steak he and Jeff had taken from the dining room the previous night. Frank would take him whatever scraps were left from the supper table.

Frank didn't like the looks of any of the three newcomers. He had recognized their type immediately: trouble-hunters, gunslicks, and probably bounty hunters, out to collect the fifteen thousand that bastard Dutton had put on his head.

Promises to be a very interesting evening, Frank thought, slipping the hammer thong off his .45, just in case.

"Find a place to sit, boys," the stationmaster called. "Or squat on the floor if you like. I'll have some food ready for you in a little while."

"Sounds great to me. But right now that coffee sure smells good," one of the men said.

"Help yourself. There's plenty. Cups hanging from hooks in the kitchen."

The three men dumped their bedrolls and saddlebags on the floor by the door, and walked over to the stove in the kitchen just off the main room. Frank was almost hidden in the shadows, and none of the three paid him any mind. Jeff was across the room, sitting on a bench, sipping his coffee in silence. He sensed something was wrong by Frank's behavior.

"Any lone riders come by today?" one of the

three toughs asked, walking back into the dining area.

"I haven't seen a soul all day. Course I ain't been lookin' neither."

The four men seated at the long table were concentrating on eating, paying no attention to anything else. The women were picking at their food. The entire group looked very road-weary.

The three toughs had taken off their heavy coats and hung them from pegs. Frank took note that the trio were all armed. Each man wore a pistol, tied down. One of them wore his pistol on the left side, butt forward for a cross-draw. Only man Frank ever knew who was fast with a cross-draw was Smoke Jensen.

Frank swallowed the last of his coffee and stepped out of the shadows, heading for the pot for another cup just as the two other toughs walked back into the main room. They stood in silence as Frank poured another cup and then stood with his back against a wall. They also took careful note that Frank held the coffee cup in his left hand. His right hand was near the butt of his .45.

"You sure look familiar," one of the man-hunters said to Frank.

"Is that right?" Frank replied.

"Where are you from?" another bounty hunter asked.

"Here and there."

"That don't tell me nothin' at all."

"Maybe it's none of your business," Frank told him.

The trio exchanged glances at that.

"Just tryin' to be friendly," the third bounty hunter said. "Goin' to be a long night. We ought to try to get along."

Frank sipped his coffee and said nothing.

The stationmaster and the stage driver were watching and listening intently, sensing trouble was building.

One of the two women was watching, her eyes on Frank. She was young and very pretty, maybe nineteen or twenty. Heart-shaped face and a pile of dark hair. Her clothing was expensive, and her little hat was about the silliest-looking thing Frank had ever seen. Useless. Wouldn't keep the rain or the sun out. Some silly fancy-pants fashion designer must have gotten drunk and gone hog-wild while working on that little noggin-topper, Frank concluded.

"It's crowded in here, boys," Frank said softly.

"For a fact," one of the man-hunters agreed.

"What's that got to do with anything?" the man standing next to him asked.

"You got any pie?" one of the traveling men asked.

"Nope," the stationmaster told him. "You just et what there was to eat."

"How about some drinking whiskey?" another traveling man inquired.

"Bar's in the next room. I'll be along to serve you."

Two of the traveling men stood up and walked into the saloon area of the stage stop/general store.

"Why don't we go in there and have a friendly drink or two?" one of the bounty hunters asked Frank.

"Not much of a drinking man," Frank replied. He held up his coffee cup. "This is fine with me."

"Good God Amighty!" the stage driver suddenly blurted out. "That's Frank Morgan!"

All eating and drinking and conversation at the table ceased and all heads turned to stare at Frank in silence.

"Evenin', folks," Frank said easily. "Don't let me disturb your meal. Go right ahead. I'll just stand here and drink my coffee."

"I knowed it was him!" one of the man-hunters said.

"Shut up, Gene," one of the others said.

"Shut up, yourself, Hal. Let's take him."

"Fifteen thousand dollars, Hal," the third man said, sticking his mouth into it. "Think about it."

"Not here, Ben, not now. Too many people."

"Fifteen thousand dollars!" the pretty lady at the table said. "What about fifteen thousand dollars?"

"See what you started, Ben?" Hal said.

"Yeah, boys," Frank said with a smile. "Tell me about this fifteen thousand dollars. That sounds real interesting. What do I have to do to earn it?"

"You a real smart-mouth, aren't you, Morgan?" Gene said.

"Forget it, Gene," Hal said.

"The hell I will! I just don't like you,

Morgan. Come to think of it, I ain't never liked you. I think all them books and such that was writ about you is all lies. I don't think you're a fast draw and I think you're a damned coward to boot. Now what do you think about that?"

"It's nice to know that you can think, but what would you know about books, Gene?" Frank asked. "You have to be able to read to know anything about books."

"I can read writin'! I shore can. What are you tryin' to say, Morgan? That I'm stupid?"

"In a word, yes," Frank replied.

"What's going on here?" the young woman at the table demanded. "I don't understand any of this."

"Shut your mouth, missy," Hal said, without taking his eyes off Frank. "This is none of your affair."

"Well!" the older woman huffed. "*You* certainly don't have any manners, you...you hooligan!"

"Oh, be quiet, you old bag!" Hal popped right back.

"Old bag!" the woman shouted.

Frank sipped his coffee and smiled at the exchange.

One of the nicely dressed men at the table rose to his feet. "Now you see here," he said to the bounty hunter. "You can't talk to Mrs. Overhouser in that manner."

"Go to hell," Hal told him.

"Overhouser?" Gene blurted out. "What the hell kind of a name is that?"

"Are you really the notorious killer Frank Morgan?" the young woman asked, looking at Frank.

"I'll admit to being Frank Morgan," Frank replied. "But I'm not a notorious killer."

"You certainly don't look like a killer to me," the young woman said.

"He ain't nothin'," Gene said, horning in on the conversation. "Big mouth, is all."

"I wasn't speaking to you," the young lady said. "I was addressing Mr. Morgan."

"Well, la-de-da," Gene said, putting one dirty hand on his hip. "Excuse the hell out of me."

"You're excused," she replied. "Now be quiet."

"Say what?" Gene said. "Don't you tell me to be quiet, you little piece of fluff!"

"Don't you dare speak to me in such a manner!" the young lady said. "I'll slap your face!"

"And I'll knock you clear into the next room, you big-mouthed heifer."

"You will do no such thing," the well-dressed traveling man said. "You...thug!"

"Sit down, Fancy Pants," Hal said. "Before you get called out."

"Out where?" the man questioned. "What are you talking about, sir?"

"That's it!" the stationmaster said, standing up. "Everybody just settle down."

"I think that's a good idea," Frank said.

"Who cares what you think?" Gene came right back. "I sure as hell don't."

Frank stepped away from the wall and positioned himself to one side of the table, putting the passengers as much out of harm's way as possible. He sensed that Gene was working himself up to pull on him.

"Hold it!" Hal said, stepping between his man and Frank. "No gunplay in here." He looked at Gene. "You sit down and have something to eat, Gene. There's always tomorrow."

"Maybe I don't want to wait until tomorrow." He looked across the room at Frank. "How about you, Morgan?"

"Too many people in this room, Gene. Too much of a risk of innocent people getting hurt."

"Then let's go outside."

"It's too cold out there, Gene. You ever been shot in real cold weather? No. Well, cold weather makes the wound hurt real bad."

"I don't plan on you woundin' me, Morgan. Now what do you think about that?"

"I don't plan on wounding you either, Gene."

"Oh?"

"No. If you're stupid enough to draw on me, I plan to kill you."

Gene cussed him, and Frank only smiled at the man. "You can cuss me all you like, partner," Frank said. "Words just bounce off of me."

"Bullets won't, you bastard!"

"Gene..." Hal said.

"Shut up! I've had it with this has-been. Draw, Morgan. Damn you, hook and draw!"

"After you, Gene," Frank softly replied.

Gene grabbed iron.

Eight

Gene was fast, but not fast enough. The man had cleared leather when Frank's bullets tore into him. Frank fired twice, the shots so close together they almost sounded as one.

Gene doubled over in shock and pain, and grabbed for the edge of a straight-backed chair for support. The chair gave way under his weight and the bounty hunter hit the floor.

"Anybody else want to get into this game?" Frank questioned, the .45 still in his hand, hammer back. A faint wisp of smoke leaked from the barrel.

"Not me, Morgan," Hal said. "But it isn't over, not by a long shot."

"I'm out of it," Ben said. "I wanna see about Gene. All right, Morgan?"

"Go ahead."

Ben knelt down beside his partner for a few seconds, then looked over at Hal. "He's done for."

"Kill that son of a bitch for me," Gene whispered. "Avenge me. Promise me you will."

"I'll get him, Gene," Ben said. "I promise you I will."

"Oh, I think I'm going to faint," the older woman said, putting the back of one hand to her forehead. "All this violence is so upsetting."

"I sure wish there was some pie for dessert," the traveling man said. "Pie always settles my stomach after a meal."

"You barbarian!" the older woman said to him. "How can you think about eating after all this violence?"

" 'Cause I'm still hungry, lady."

Gene groaned once and died.

Hal and Ben looked around the room. The stationmaster and the driver were standing with shotguns in their hands, the hammers eared back.

"No trouble, boys," Hal said. "You have my word on that."

"This is the most exciting thing I have ever seen," the young lady said, wriggling her butt on the bench. "It's so...well, *thrilling*."

"Somebody drag that body out of here," another traveling man said.

"Stick him in the shed," the stage driver said. "He'll keep 'til mornin'."

"How disgusting!" the older lady said. She looked at the younger woman. "And you're just *awful*, thinking any of this was thrilling!"

"Oh, shut up, lady," Ben said. "Come on, Hal, help me with Gene. We'll tote him outside."

Frank stood quietly and reloaded while Gene's buddies carried him outside. He tossed the brass empties into a trash barrel and walked over to the coffeepot, pouring another cup. Then he sat down on a bench.

"Are you goin' to have any supper, Mr. Morgan?" the stationmaster asked, propping his shotgun against a wall.

"I'll probably have a bite after a while."

"I'll get a mop and clean up the mess on the floor," the stage driver said.

"I still feel faint," the older woman complained. "I need to lie down and collect myself."

"Pick a spot on the floor, lady," the stationmaster said. "This ain't no hotel."

"I shall certainly post a letter of grievance to the owners of this stage line," she told him. "The treatment I'm receiving is deplorable."

"Mr. Morgan," the young woman said to Frank. "I have aspirations of becoming a writer. I would like to talk with you at some future point...with your permission, of course."

Crap! Frank thought. But he nodded his head in agreement.

Then he remembered the writer Louis Pettigrew, the little Boston author of all those ridiculous dime novels about him, and Frank suppressed a shudder. Louis had promised to follow him no matter where he went and write his life's story. God, what if Frank had *two* writers following him around!

He looked at the very attractive young woman. Naw! No way could this pretty little thing manage to follow him around during his wanderings.

Oh, hell! Frank thought, as the young lady got to her feet. *Now she's going to come over here and sit down beside me.*

"Now just where do you think you're going, Colleen?" the older woman asked.

"To sit beside Mr. Morgan."

"Oh, no, you most certainly will do no such thing! Why...the man is a craven killer!"

"Stuff and nonsense, Martha. The man protected himself, that's all."

"You come back here!"

Colleen walked over and sat down beside Frank. "Do you mind, Mr. Morgan?"

"Not at all, miss." *Damn!*

Colleen sat down and said, "I've read all the books about you and Mr. MacCallister and the mysterious gunfighter called Smoke Jensen. Do you know any of those men, Mr. Morgan?"

"Jenson or Falcon MacCallister?"

"Either one."

"Know both of them. *Knew* Falcon. He's dead now. Killed by ambush and buried 'side his wife overlooking MacCallister's Valley."

"But Jenson is still alive, isn't he?"

"Last I heard he was."

"Who is that handsome young man with you, sir?"

Aha! She's got eyes for Jeff, Frank thought. *Good. Get those two hooked up and I'll be shut of both of them.* "That's Jeff Barton. He's from New York City."

"Are you all right over there, Colleen?" the older, rather ample woman hollered.

"Of course I'm all right, Martha. You're looking right at me."

"Who is that woman?" Frank asked. "Kin of yours?"

74

"Oh, no. That's Mrs. Martha Overhouser. She is a recent widow. Her husband died suddenly."

"I'm sure he's resting much better now."

That comment blew right past Colleen. "She has a brother out in California. That's where she's going."

"This way? Last time I checked, California was west of Denver, not south."

Colleen giggled. "Oh, you silly! No. She has a friend in Durango. She's going to visit her for a time. They haven't seen each other in years."

"I see."

"They were friends in finishing school. Back in Massachusetts. She's looking forward to seeing Mrs. Tremaine."

Frank had just taken a sip of coffee, and almost choked on it. "Mrs. Tremaine?"

"Yes. Paulette Tremaine."

Frank coughed a couple of times and cleared his throat. "Does your friend know what Mrs. Tremaine does for a living?"

"I really don't know. She told me that Paulette's husband died about fifteen years ago and about five years ago she moved to Durango and is operating a very successful business there."

Paulette Tremaine got run out of Denver about five years ago, Frank recalled, hiding his smile. Mrs. Martha Overhouser was in for one hell of a surprise, for Paulette operated one of the West's most notorious whorehouses, and had for just about fifteen years. After she wore out her welcome, among other

75

things, in Denver, she moved her entire operation to Durango. As far as Paulette's husband's dying, he sure did that: She shot him five times after she caught him stark naked with another woman, on the floor of their fine home in the fashionable section of Denver. Paulette had about twenty soiled doves in her employ. Something for everyone's tastes, so the story went.

"Martha is a big supporter of the Temperance Movement, Mr. Morgan. She is going to spread the word about the evils of drinking here in the West."

"Oh?"

"Yes. And that's not all."

"I was afraid of that."

"Martha is active in a movement that would give women the vote."

Hal and Ben walked back into the room, a blast of cold wind signaling their entrance. "We put Gene in the shed," Hal said. "Don't seem decent, though. Me and Gene been together for a long time."

"He won't mind being in the shed," one of the traveling men said.

Ben looked at him, an ugly expression on his face. "Who the hell asked you?"

The traveling man shrugged his shoulders and looked away.

Mrs. Overhouser stood up and walked over to Colleen. She held out a hand. "Come, Colleen. I've found us a place to sleep for tonight. One that will provide some privacy." She gave Frank a very dirty look.

"Go on, Colleen," Frank said softly, his eyes not leaving Ben's face. "I think there's going to be some more trouble in here."

"But..." Colleen started to protest.

"Go on," Frank said more firmly. "Jeff," he called. "Come escort the ladies out of here."

The traveling men, still seated at the table, rose and went into the small bar area of the stage stop.

Frank stood up to face the remaining bounty hunters. "You boys just won't let it alone, will you?"

"You can't get both of us, Morgan," Hal said. "Just ain't no way that's possible."

"Now wait a minute here!" the station-master protested, reaching for his shotgun.

"You touch that scattergun and you're dead, mister," Ben said.

"The same goes for you," Hal told the driver. "Just back off and mind your own business."

"What the hell are you talking about? This place is my business!" the stationmaster protested.

"And this is our business," Hal told him. "That gunslinger standin' right there." He looked at Frank.

"Yeah. Me and Hal done talked it over. Gene ain't gonna die for nothin'," Ben said, his eyes never leaving Frank. "Me and him was close as brothers. So it's *root, hog, or die* time. You understand that, Morgan?"

"I hear you."

"We gonna make sure them women is safe

77

away from stray bullets," Hal said. "I don't give a damn 'bout the men. See to that," he told the driver and the stationmaster. "Go on, make yourselves useful."

"You ready, Morgan?" Ben said.

"Do I have a choice?"

"Not none at all."

"Lots of lead going to fly in this building, Ben. And there are a lot of people in here."

"I done told 'em to hunt a hole. They don't, that there ain't no worry of mine."

"You're all heart, Ben."

"Huh?"

Frank watched Hal edge a few steps to his left. "Stand still, bounty hunter."

"I got a better idea, Morgan," Ben said. "Draw!"

Both man-hunters grabbed iron.

Nine

Frank drew, fired, and jumped to one side all in one smooth movement. His first shot hit Hal in the shoulder and knocked the bounty hunter back. Frank hit the floor just as he fired again. The impact with the floor threw his aim off, and his bullet struck Ben in the hip and the man collapsed to the floor.

Martha and Colleen began screaming from the saloon side of the stage stop, joining in with the shouting and cussing of the traveling men.

Hal crawled to his feet and banged a shot in Frank's direction, the bullet thudding into the wall behind where Frank was kneeling on the floor.

Frank snapped off a round just as Hal dropped to the floor. The bullet knocked a chunk out of the wall.

Cussing loudly, Ben fired, his round missing Frank by several feet. Frank returned the fire and did not miss. Ben was slammed backward, a hole in the center of his forehead, his eyes wide open, a startled expression on his face.

Hal staggered to his feet, and this time Frank's aim was on the mark. Hal fell back against the wall, his heart shattered. He slid down to the floor, his pistol falling from suddenly dead fingers.

Frank rose wearily to his feet and reloaded as the big room began filling with people.

"Damnedest thing I ever seen," the stage driver said.

"I damn shore never seen nothin' like it," the stationmaster said.

"This is terrible!" Martha Overhouser bellowed. "I shall never ride this stage line again."

"Good," the driver told her. "That's the best news I've heard in weeks. You ain't done nothin' but moan and complain all the way."

"Don't you speak to me in that tone of voice, you lout!" Martha hollered.

"Come on," Frank said. "I'll help you carry the bodies out to the shed."

"Why don't you stay out there with them, the both of you," Martha yelled.

"Ain't she a sight to behold?" the driver said to Frank.

Frank said nothing, just shook his head.

Frank and the driver stored the bodies in the shed, and the driver said, "They just might stay here for several months, you know? They get good and froze, they'll keep 'til spring."

"That'll be a lovely sight, for sure."

"Won't it, though."

"You want their guns?" Frank asked.

"Naw. I got me a good pistol and a fine rifle I carry on my runs. That's all I need. Got several more of each at the house. Don't need no more. But thanks for offerin'."

"I'll help you fix that axle come daylight."

"That's white of you, Mr. Morgan. I'll take you up on that too."

"I'll be around."

After the driver left, Frank went through the pockets of the man-hunters. He found some cash, and would give that to Jeff. He took their guns, carried them back into the stage stop, and hung the belts on pegs.

"How many men does that make you've shot dead, Mr. Gunfighter?" Martha asked.

Frank did not reply. He had had just about all he was going to take of Mrs. Overhouser.

"That's not fair, Martha," Colleen said. "All Mr. Morgan did was defend himself. He didn't start the trouble."

Martha snorted her contempt at that.

Frank poured a fresh cup of coffee and sat down at the table. He was suddenly very tired.

"You want me to fix you a plate of food?" Colleen asked.

"Not now, miss. I'll maybe get something later. But thank you."

"Well...I'm going to try to get some rest. Good night."

"Night, miss."

Frank sat at the table for a long time, drinking coffee. The only way he could get the bounty on him lifted was to get rid of Lawyer Dutton. But Frank doubted that Dutton would ever again come west of the Mississippi. So that left him...

"Living with a fifteen-thousand-dollar bounty on my head," he muttered.

He finished his coffee and looked around him. People were sleeping all over the station. Frank went into the kitchen and found some scraps of food, and took them outside for Dog. After checking on the horses and making certain Dog's water bucket was full, he returned to the station and spread his blankets on the floor and went to sleep.

Frank was the first one up. He quietly built up the fire in the kitchen stove and filled up the big coffeepot with water; then while he waited for the water to boil, he got a fire going in the fireplace. He then went outside and got Dog, bringing him into the station. He fed the animal some cold biscuits he'd found, gave him some water, and Dog promptly curled up in a corner and went to sleep.

Colleen had been watching Frank from the

darkness of the room. "You take good care of that dog," she remarked.

"People who abuse animals have a serious flaw," Frank replied. "At least that's my opinion."

"And you're an educated man too."

"Not really. I just like to read."

"Is that the exception or the rule in the West?"

"For men who can read, I think it's pretty much the rule. For years we were hungry for news out here. Men would pass newspapers around until they were worn out. News might be weeks or months old, but it was still news."

"Jeff told me you were going to Durango."

"That's the plan."

"Then we might see each other again in the town?"

"Could be. It isn't a city by any means."

"Mr. Morgan...what exactly do you do for a living?"

Frank smiled. "I try to stay alive, miss."

"Then you are a man of some means?"

"I suppose you could say that."

"Forgive my questions, Mr. Morgan, but I am the curious type."

"Person can't learn anything except by listening and asking questions, miss."

"Colleen, please."

"All right."

"Does Durango have a newspaper, Mr. Morgan?"

"Frank."

"All right, Frank."

"I don't know about any newspaper. Might have a weekly. Why?"

"I told you. I want to be a writer. I would like to apply for a job."

"A woman reporter? I never heard of such a thing. Menfolks might not take too kindly to that."

"Women are on the move in this nation, Frank. You men better get used to it."

Frank chuckled softly. "I reckon so, Colleen."

Frank helped the driver and stationmaster replace the broken axle, and the stage pulled out just before ten o'clock. The heavy snowstorm had passed and the temperature had warmed up; most of the snow had melted where the rays of the sun could touch it.

"I told Colleen I'd try to find her when we got to Durango," Jeff said.

"Oh?"

"Yes. She's a very sweet young lady."

"Really? I didn't notice."

"You're getting old, Frank."

"That must be it. Come on."

"Where are we going?"

"To bury Gene, Hal, and Ben."

"What about their horses?"

"We'll take them with us. Sell them along the way."

"We're going over the mountains?"

"No. Too risky this time of year. That snowstorm might be sign of a really bad storm coming. We'll stay with the roads. It's longer, but safer."

"A harbinger."

"A what?"

"A sign of things to come. Like, oh, a harbinger of doom."

"Right. I'll have to remember that. A harbinger of doom. Sounds grim."

"It usually is."

The men got shovels out of the shed, and the bodies of the three man-hunters were buried about a hundred yards behind the stage stop. Frank and Jeff lined the outside of their graves with rocks.

"That's about all we can do, I reckon," Frank said. "Come on. Let's get packed up and hit the trail."

Three days of steady riding brought the men to the center of the San Luis Valley. There Frank headed them west, and they stopped at midday in a small settlement west of Alamosa.

"We'll sell these horses and gear here," Frank said.

"I want another hot bath," Jeff said.

"You just had one a few days ago," Frank replied with a smile.

Jeff looked at his saddle partner to see if he was kidding. Frank was. "You're no rose yourself, Frank. Dog's the cleanest of us all."

"I won't argue that."

"Fine-lookin' horses, mister," the owner of the local livery said. "And the saddles are in good shape too. How do I know them animals ain't stolen?"

Frank stared at the man for a few seconds. The livery man suddenly became edgy. "But I'm sure they ain't," the man added finally.

"Mister," Frank spoke very softly, "my name is Frank Morgan. I have never stolen anything in my life. Is that good enough for you?"

"Frank Morgan," the livery man repeated. He licked very dry lips. "Yeah. I seen your pitcher a bunch of times. That's who you is, for a fact."

"How much for the horses and gear?"

The livery man very quickly named a very fair price, and Frank accepted it.

"You got a good deal," Frank told him, making out a bill of sale.

"I 'spect I did. What happened to the original owners?"

"They're dead and in the ground."

"I figured as much. You didn't cut 'em no slack, huh?"

"Just enough to get them killed."

"Ah...you stayin' in town long, Mr. Morgan?"

Frank smiled. "Just long enough to have a bath and buy some things."

"Good. Bathhouse is over yonder." He pointed. "Have a good wash and do come back sometime."

"Sarcastic fellow," Jeff remarked as they walked away.

"Story of my life, Jeff. I stopped letting it bother me years ago. But he offered us a good price for the horses and gear. The money's yours. You'll have a nice reserve of money to get you started in something in Durango."

"It was my lucky day when I ran into you, Frank."

"Don't be too sure. The trip ain't over yet."

Ten

Frank and Jeff did not leave immediately after their bath. Instead, they bought rooms at the town's only hotel. The town marshal showed up at Frank's door within ten minutes after the men had signed in. He wasn't taking any chances with Frank Morgan, he was carrying a Greener: a double-barreled sawed-off shotgun.

"Relax, Marshal," Frank told him. "I'm not trouble-hunting in your town."

The marshal eyeballed him suspiciously. "Trouble follows you, Morgan. What are you doing here?"

"Getting tired of questions, for one thing."

"Part of my job is asking questions. So I'll ask it again: What are you doing in this town?"

"Well, I had me a bath, and now I'm going to go out and get me a bite to eat. Then I'm going to bed and get a good night's sleep."

The marshal stared at him for a moment. "Morgan, there's a bounty on your head. Are you aware of that?"

"Oh, yes."

"Then I'll tell you something else: There are two gunslicks in town. Rode in this morning. I've heard of them both. Their guns are for hire and they aren't above killing an innocent man for a big enough bounty. I hear the bounty on you is fifteen thousand dollars."

"That's right."

"You're going to have every man-hunter west of the Mississippi River after you, Morgan."

"Probably."

"I don't want any showdowns in my town."

"I hope there won't be any, Marshal. But I intend to have supper and then spend the night in your town. I hope to do all that peacefully. But if you've got some trouble-hunters here looking to brace me...that's their problem, not mine."

The marshal sighed in frustration. "I've done all I can under the law. You've been warned, Morgan," he said, then turned and walked away.

"Indeed I have," Frank muttered.

Frank took Dog out back of the hotel for a walk, then returned to the room and fed him. Dog ate, and then lay down on the rug beside the bed and went to sleep.

Shadows were lengthening when Frank and Jeff stepped outside to stand on the covered porch of the hotel.

"Fellow in the lobby told me that cafe across the street serves a good meal," Jeff said. "You hungry?"

"I sure am."

"There are two men watching us real hard from down the street."

"I see them."

"Trouble?"

"Probably. We'll see. Those are more than likely the two gunslicks the marshal mentioned. It's a free country; they can stare at us if they like. Right now, let's go get us some supper."

After a supper of beef, beans, potatoes, hot bread, a big wedge of pie, and a pot of coffee, Frank and Jeff paused on the boardwalk. Frank rolled a smoke and stared for a moment into the gloom of early evening.

Jeff patted his stomach. "That was good. Can I borrow one of your books and read for a while?"

"Help yourself, Jeff. I'm going to walk over to the saloon and listen to the talk."

"Frank, those trouble-hunters will probably be waiting for you."

"Probably so. But I don't live my life for other people. I'll do what I damn well please to do, when I damn well please to do it."

Frank pushed open the door and stepped into the warm and smoky saloon. A blast of cold air entered with him, and a number of heads turned as the air hit them. Most turned back to their cards, conversation, or drinks...a few did not. Among those that did not were two tough-looking men standing at the end of the bar and two young men seated at a table.

"Morgan," Frank heard one of the young men say.

Damn! Frank thought. *I can handle the two man-hunters. I didn't count on the two punks. Maybe they're nothing but a couple of loud-mouths and nothing more.*

But he doubted it. He had a strong feeling the two young men were hunting a reputation.

Frank walked slowly to the nearest spot at the bar and waited for the very reluctant bartender to walk over. Frank finally called for a beer.

"Just wait your turn, Morgan," one of the young men shouted. "You ain't nothin' special 'round here."

Frank ignored the punk.

"You hear me, old man?" the punk shouted.

"I think he's deef," his loudmouthed partner said with a laugh.

Frank sipped his beer and remained silent.

Frank cut his eyes and watched as the town marshal walked in and stepped to one side, staying in the shadows close to the front door.

No one in the big room seemed to notice as the marshal remained silent and watchful.

The two bounty hunters at the far end of the bar watched Frank, but made no hostile moves. The older of the two seemed slightly amused at the antics of the loudmouthed young men.

Frank rolled a cigarette and popped a match into flame with his left hand. His right hand remained a few inches from the butt of his .45.

"You're a long way from home, Morgan," the younger of the bounty hunters called.

Frank looked at him but said nothing.

"I heard he had turned yeller, hung up his guns, and was squatting in a shack up north of here," one of the young men declared.

"Shut up, Max," the marshal said. "Before your butt overloads your mouth."

"I ain't broke no laws, Marshal," the young man said. "You ain't got no call to come down on me."

"I'm trying to save your life."

"From this old, wore-out, gray-headed has-been? Don't make me laugh."

"He ain't no has-been," the other loud-mouth said with a chuckle. "He's a never-was!"

"Suit yourselves, boys," the marshal responded. "You've been warned."

The older of the bounty hunters moved a few feet from his partner, stepping from the bar.

"The outhouse is through that door behind you," the bartender told him.

"Shut up," the man-hunter told him.

Frank waited.

"Morgan!" the man-hunter called. "Look at me, Morgan."

Frank cut his eyes.

"I'm thinkin' it's time for me to call your reputation."

Frank smiled at that. Using his left hand, he raised his beer mug and took a sip.

"Did you hear me, Morgan?"

"Everyone in the room did," Frank replied calmly, placing his mug back on the bar.

"Well?"

"Well, what?"

"What are you going to do about it, damn you!"

Frank took a deep drag on his cigarette and dropped it to the floor, toeing it out with his boot. "Nothing," he said.

"You're a coward, Morgan!"

"And you're a fool, whoever you are."

"Huh?"

"And hard of hearing too."

Max stood up, pushing his chair back. "I think I'll just buy into this game," he said.

"This is no game, boy," Frank told him. "I would advise you to sit down and think about that."

"I don't take no orders from you, Morgan."

"Suit yourself, boy. It's your life to live." He cut his eyes to the man-hunter. "What's your name?"

"I'm Phil. My buddy's name is Ned. Why?"

"Something has to be carved on your grave marker." He smiled. "Or markers."

Phil frowned, and then called Frank a couple of very vulgar names. He stepped further away from the bar, his hand hovering near the butt of his pistol. "You ready, Morgan?"

"For what, Phil?"

"Damn you, Morgan! You know what."

"Tell me. My memory's getting real bad in my old age."

Phil glared at him in disgust. "What does it take to make you fight, Morgan?"

"Hell, I didn't come in here looking for a fight. I came in here for a quiet drink and some intelligent conversation. I found my drink, but the conversation so far is something less than intelligent."

Phil thought about that for a few seconds. "Are you callin' me stupid, Morgan?"

"Well, now that you mention it, I guess I am."

"You sorry piece of coyote crap! I don't take that kind of talk from nobody."

"Well, Phil, old partner, I guess you'll have to take it. 'Cause if you pull on me, I'm going to kill you. And that's the way it is."

"Take it outside, boys," the barkeep said.

"Too cold out there," Frank told him. "Wind is picking up and it's mighty harsh. I like it in here."

"Well, now, I reckon you've made it clear where you stand, Morgan," Phil said. "You've threatened to kill me. I got to pick up the challenge."

"Only if you're a fool."

"By God, I wouldn't take that insult from nobody!" Max said, stepping away from the table.

Frank sighed and stepped away from the bar. There was little time left for conversation. "I'm not talking to you, boy. You best sit your butt back down in that chair and be quiet."

"I don't take no orders from you neither, old man," Max said. "You hear that?"

"Yeah, I heard it, kid." Frank did not take his eyes off Phil.

"I'm callin' you, Morgan!" Max shouted, his voice rising in nervousness.

"Your mama's calling you, boy," Frank told him. "Was I you, I'd think about that."

"To hell with my mama and to hell with you!" Max said.

"You ought to be ashamed of yourself for saying that about your mother," Frank told him.

"I've had all this crap I'm goin' to take!" the young man shouted. "Draw, Morgan!"

Max went for his gun.

Eleven

Frank's shot was perfectly placed, striking the young man in the right shoulder and knocking him back. The pistol slipped from his suddenly numb hand. Max stumbled into a table and put his left hand out for support. The table tilted under his weight and slid out from under him. Max hit the floor and lay there, groaning in pain.

Frank stepped to one side and pumped two rounds into Phil, who had dragged iron just a second behind Max's unsuccessful effort. Phil staggered backward and tried to lift his .45. His right arm refused to comply with his brain's wishes. Phil squeezed the trigger and the hammer fell. The shot blew off the front part of his right foot and the bounty hunter went down hard on the floor, howling in shock and pain.

Ned held up both hands. "I'm out of this!" he hollered.

"Don't shoot, Morgan!" the young man who was seated with Max yelled. "I ain't havin' none of this."

"You bastard!" Phil said, both hands holding his perforated belly. "You done killed me."

"For sure he's gonna save on boots from now on," the barkeep said, peering over the counter at Phil's ruined foot.

Frank slid his .45 back into leather and waited.

"That's it," the marshal said, stepping out of the shadows and walking toward the fallen Max. "Everyone stand easy."

"I'll get the doc," a man said, standing up and heading for the door. "If he's sober, that is."

"Do that," the marshal said. "Drag him over here if he's drunk."

"Help me!" Max called, waving his one good arm. "Oh, Lord, I believe I'm done for."

"Oh, shut up, Max," the marshal told him after taking a quick look. "You got plugged in the shoulder, that's all. Somebody else will have to kill you."

"Somebody probably will, for a fact," a patron commented.

"Oh, I cain't stand the pain!" Max complained. "I'm hurtin' something fierce."

Frank picked up his beer mug with his left hand and took a healthy gulp, easing the dryness in his throat. He motioned for the barkeep to refill it.

"Is it gettin' dark?" Phil called. "I can't see too well no more."

Frank took a sip of his freshly pulled beer and said nothing.

"Oh, Lordy, I'm hurtin'!" Max hollered.

"Good," Frank said. "Maybe it will make you think the next time you want to drag iron against someone."

"I hate you, Morgan!" Max hollered.

"I'm brokenhearted, son. I'll probably lose at least a minute of sleep over it."

Several of the patrons snickered at that.

"You old farts think this is funny?" Max shouted. "Damn you all to hell!"

That prompted more laughter.

"Don't nobody care 'bout me?" Phil said. "I'm goin' to die and don't nobody give a damn."

"You got that right," the barkeep told him. "You got my floor all messed up."

The town's doctor came in. He appeared sober, but Frank could tell the man was a boozer: His nose was red as a beet and spiderwebbed with broken veins. He knelt down beside Max and ripped open his shirt.

"Sit him up," the doc said. He looked at the exit wound in the young man's back. "He'll live."

"Is that all you got to say?" Max yelped. "Give me something for the pain."

"Later," the doc told him. "You can stand it, boy. Hell, the way you been strutting around town, I guessed you were tough as wang leather."

"I'm tough, Doc. But I also hurt like thunder."

"You'll make it." The doc moved over to Phil and checked his wounds.

"I'm done for, ain't I, Doc?" Phil asked.

"You sure are."

"Well, hell, Doc! You don't have to say it like that."

"How else is there to say it? You've taken your last ride. You're not long for this world. You're going to croak. Is that better?"

"Hell, no!"

"You want me to get a preacher?"

"Why?"

"To help you make your peace with the Almighty."

Phil coughed for a few seconds. "I don't need no sky-talker. I want you to dig these bullets out and get me well."

"You're lung-shot, fellow. And it looks like the other bullet poked a hole in your gizzard."

"You ain't much help, Doc."

"I don't have a lot to work with, fellow. Are you in a lot of pain?"

"Hell, yes."

The doctor reached into his bag and hauled out a bottle of laudanum. "Give me a spoon," he told the barkeep.

"A clean one?"

"It doesn't make any difference."

"Oh, Lord," Phil moaned.

Jeff walked into the saloon with a group of other curious citizens and strolled over to Frank. "Are you all right?"

"I'm fine, Jeff. How's Dog?"

"Sleeping. These the bounty hunters?"

"One of them. The other one is a kid with a big mouth."

"I heard the shooting. A deputy wouldn't let us in; kept us outside for several minutes."

"Can I put my arms down now?" Ned asked the marshal.

"Put your arms down and get the hell out of town," the marshal told him.

"Now?"

"Right now."

"Man, it's freezin' cold out there. My horse is tired. Hell, I ain't done nothin'. 'Sides, I got to see about gettin' my buddy buried."

"I ain't dead yet, goddamnit!" Phil groaned.

"You will be 'fore long," the doctor told him.

"Thanks a lot," Phil said.

"You're welcome." The doctor stood up. "I've done all that I can do."

"Hell, you ain't done nothin'!" Phil said.

"It's still all I can do."

"Wonderful," Phil said weakly. He focused his eyes on Morgan, standing at the bar. "I hope you get gut-shot, Drifter. I hope you die hard, you bastard."

"Drifter?" the doctor questioned.

"That's what some has taken to calling Frank Morgan," the marshal said.

The doctor looked at Frank. "Are you really Frank Morgan?"

"Yes."

"I've been reading about you in an Eastern newspaper I get sent out here."

"From Boston?" Frank asked.

"Yes. How did you know?"

"Articles written by Louis Pettigrew?"

"That's the man's name."

"Don't believe everything you read." Frank met the marshal's steady gaze. "You through with me?"

"I sure as hell hope so."

Frank drained his beer mug. "Come on, Jeff. Let's go back to the hotel."

"Morgan, I want you out of town come daylight," the marshal said.

"We'll be gone. Count on it."

"What about me?" Phil said.

"You'll be gone come morning," the doctor told him. "And you can count on that too."

"You 'bout the sorriest damn doctor I ever seen," Phil told him.

"Feel free to mention that to God," the doctor said. He paused and added, "Or the Devil."

Frank and Jeff were saddled up and ready to ride out just after dawn the next morning. Frank stepped out of the barn into the daylight for a look around. The first person he saw standing in the middle of the street was Ned.

"You, Morgan!" the man-hunter called. "My partner Phil just died."

"He brought it on himself."

"He'll soon be cold in the ground and you're walkin' around. That don't seem right to me."

"Seems fine to me."

"You a smart-aleck bastard, Morgan. Makin' light of my partner's dyin'."

"I'm riding out, Ned. Leaving town. So get out of the way. I'm not looking for trouble."

"I'm fixin' to give you more trouble than you can handle, Morgan."

"I don't want a fight, Ned."

"I do."

The marshal had stepped out of a cafe and was standing under the awning, listening. Listening and watching, but making no attempt to interfere. He had just finished breakfast and was leaning up against a support post, picking his teeth.

"Go on with your life, Ned. Go away and live to be an old man. Don't prod me anymore."

"Can't do that, Morgan. It's the code."

"The code? What damn code?"

"Mine and Phil's. We promised to avenge each other if something was to happen." Ned took a couple of steps closer, his right hand close to the butt of his pistol.

"Don't do this, Ned. I'm telling you, man, it isn't worth it."

"It's got to be, Morgan. I know Phil would have done the same for me."

Morgan quickly cut his eyes toward the marshal. But he knew the marshal would not interfere. The West was slowly being civilized, and courtrooms and law books were being used more and more. In many places, legal words and phrases filled the air instead of gun smoke, but this was still the West, and men still settled quarrels with guns.

"I can shoot him from here," Jeff said softly, standing in the door of the livery, holding a rifle.

"Stay out of it," Frank told him. "I hope you never have to kill a man."

"I'm here if you need me."

"All right."

"Who you talkin' to, Morgan?" Ned called.

"The ghosts of dead bounty hunters."

"Huh?"

"I'm getting very weary of this, Ned. I'm trying to ride out and you're standing in my way."

"One way to move me, Morgan. And you know what that is."

"I guess that's the way it has to be," Frank said, resignation in his voice.

The marshal tossed his toothpick into the street and hitched at his gunbelt.

"You stay out of this, Marshal!" Ned shouted. "This ain't none of your affair." Ned took a couple more steps toward Frank. "I'll kill you where you stand, Morgan. Hook and draw, you son of a bitch!"

"After you, Ned."

Ned's right hand hovered over the butt of his pistol.

"Having second thoughts, Ned?" Frank asked. "I would, were I you."

"You ain't me!"

"For a fact. Ned?"

"What?"

"You got enough money on you to pay for your burying?"

"Hell with you, Morgan. I'm gonna have plenty of money once you're down."

"Think about it, man. Walk away and live."

"I got a better idea, Morgan. Draw!"

Twelve

Ned was knocked to the ground when Frank's bullet slammed into the bounty hunter's hip...exactly where Frank had intended the .45-caliber slug to strike. Ned lost his grip on his pistol. The marshal was in the center of the street before Ned could grab his pistol. He kicked the gun away.

"It's over, mister," the marshal told him. "The Drifter let you live. Be thankful for that and let it go."

"I'll kill him someday!"

"You're a fool."

Jeff led the horses outside and Frank mounted up. Dog was in his pouch on the side of the pack animal, only his head poking out of the pouch, safe and comfortable, taking in all the sights.

"I'll kill you someday, Drifter!" Ned hollered.

Frank ignored the threat and lifted a hand in farewell to the marshal.

"Good luck, Drifter," the marshal called.

"I need me a doctor!" Ned hollered. "And get me somebody 'sides that damn quack that fumbled around and let Phil die. You hear me? I'm gonna kill you, Morgan!" he shouted. "Damn you! That there's a promise. You can count on it."

Frank and Jeff rode out of town without looking back. Jeff did not say anything about the daybreak shooting, and Frank never mentioned it. But for several hours after riding out of the town Jeff looked often over his shoulder, checking their back trail.

In the mid-1880's Durango was a rip-roaring, wide-open town, with saloons operating twenty-four hours a day and "shady ladies" offering their favors quite openly.

"Oh, my God!" Jeff said, as the pair reined up on the outskirts of the mining town and Jeff got his first close-up look at Durango. "Are those men laying in the street dead?"

"No. Just drunk and passed out. Come on. Let's stable our horses and check this place out."

"I would like to have a bath. As a matter of fact, both of us could use a bath."

"You think you might run into Colleen?" Frank asked with a smile.

"Dog smells better than we do," Jeff replied, avoiding the question.

"It would be my luck to run into Martha Overhouser," Frank said, lifting the reins.

Jeff was still laughing as they reined up in front of the nearest livery.

Durango was in its heyday, and the town was still growing, but the growing pains would ease up a lot over the next few years. By the early

1900's, Durango would fall on hard times as the mines began to play out.

The first thing Frank noticed was a freshly painted sign hanging outside a new building: "The Henson Company."

The boy sure doesn't let any grass grow under his feet when it comes to business, Frank thought. Then he smiled secretly, inwardly, thinking: *The more money you make, son, the more money I make.* That thought amused him.

"You have a funny look on your face, Frank," Jeff said. "Kind of like the cat who ate the cream."

"Nothing important, Jeff. Come on. Let's find us a place in one of the hotels."

"And if we can't?"

"Then we'll find us a shack outside of town and live there."

There was no room in any of the hotels nor in any of the rooming houses, and it was late in the day.

"We'll sleep in the livery," Frank said. "Up in the loft. Tomorrow we'll have our baths."

"When do we get something to eat? I'm hungry."

"Right now, if you're that hungry."

"I am."

The men found a cafe and had supper: beef, beans, potatoes, bread, and a piece of pie. Frank got a big sackful of scraps for Dog.

"I feel better," Jeff declared as the men stepped out onto the boardwalk.

"You should feel terrible. You ate enough for two people."

Jeff belched. "Excuse me."

On the way back to the livery, the men approached the marshal, walking the boardwalk. The marshal paused and looked hard at Frank for a long moment. Frank watched the man's face tighten and his eyes narrow as he recognized him.

"Evening, Marshal," Frank greeted him.

The man nodded his head, still not quite sure he was looking at the legendary gun-handler.

Frank gave the sack of scraps to Jeff. "Feed Dog, will you, Jeff. I'll be along in a few minutes."

"Sure. I want to pull off my boots and wriggle my toes for a while anyway.

Frank pulled out the makings and rolled a smoke, then offered the sack and papers to the marshal. "Smoke, Marshal?"

"Don't mind if I do." Rolling his cigarette, the marshal asked, "Are my eyes playing tricks on me? Are you really Frank Morgan?"

"In person."

"Damn!"

"I'm not here to cause any trouble."

"I'm sure you've heard this before, Morgan: Trouble follows you."

"I've heard it a time or two."

The marshal popped a match into flame, lit his cigarette, and waited.

"Marshal, I met up with a young fellow wandering around on the trail. He was from New York City, first time out here, and was lost as a goose. I told him he could ride along with me. That's all there is to my being here."

"I believe you, Morgan. But it still puts you here. You know, I reckon, about the bounty on your head?"

"I know."

"Fifteen thousand dollars is a lot of money."

"For a fact."

"This town is full of trouble-hunters. When the word gets around that you're here, and it will, real quick, there'll be men looking to call you out. And not just for the bounty. There are always some who'll be hunting a reputation. I'd say the same thing to Smoke Jensen, Falcon MacCallister, Louis Longmont, and a dozen other fast guns."

"I know, and I don't blame you."

"But you're still going to stay here in Durango?"

"I am."

"I figured you'd say that. How long are you going to be in town, Morgan?"

"Quite a spell."

"I figured you'd say that too. Well, I reckon I'd better tell the undertaker to get ready for some business."

"Not necessarily. I won't start any trouble."

"But you won't back down from any either?"

"I'll do my very best to try to talk my way out of it, if possible. But I won't back down from any man. I never have and I never will."

"That's about all I can hope for, I guess."

"That's best I can do."

"All right, Morgan. I'll take your word for it. You seem like a straight shooter to me." The marshal smiled faintly. "Bad choice of words, wasn't it? Anyway, welcome to Durango." He brushed by Frank and walked on down the boardwalk.

"Seems like a nice enough fellow," Frank muttered. He looked across the busy street and met the eyes of his son, Conrad. Frank lifted a hand in greeting. Conrad stared at him for a moment, then turned away without acknowledging the greeting in any way.

Boy blames me for getting his mother killed, Frank thought. *Well, he'll either come around to thinking straight, or he won't. There isn't a damn thing I can do about it.*

Frank felt eyes on him and looked down the street. The marshal was watching him. Frank held up a hand, signaling the marshal to wait, and walked down toward him.

"Got a question for you, Marshal."

"All right."

"The Pine and Vanbergen gangs around?"

"I heard about that woman getting killed up north a few months back, and I also heard she was your ex-wife. Any truth in that?"

"Yes."

The marshal sighed. "Oh, brother. Word around town is that young uppity rich dude, Conrad Browning, is your son. Any truth in that?"

"Yes. Although I'm sure it would hurt Conrad's mouth to admit it."

"I...guess I understand that."

"He didn't know until a few months ago."

"Ahh. Well, in answer to your question, yes, the Pine and Vanbergen gangs are around.

But Vic and Ned never come into town. At least I've never seen either of them come in."

"You can expect them to now."

"Because of you?"

"Yes."

The marshal frowned and then shrugged his shoulders. "You have any more good news you want to tell me?"

"The gangs just might be after Conrad too."

"Have you seen those bodyguards of his?"

"Two of them."

"He has four. Big bruisers."

"But they're not Western men."

The marshal gave that a few seconds' thought. "No, they're not. I see what you mean."

"They're not going to react the same."

"No. Probably not. Damn! I'll have to keep an eye on young Browning's girlfriend too."

"Conrad has a girlfriend?"

"Yes. She came to town a few days ago on the stage. From back East somewhere. The two young people seemed to hit it right off...even though personally I think Conrad is a stuck-up, fancy-pants little turd. She's a real pretty little thing. Colleen something or another."

"Well, it certainly didn't take her long to find herself a beau," Jeff remarked after Frank broke the news to him.

"Conrad has a good eye for the ladies," Frank said.

Jeff sighed as the two men prepared for sleep on the hay in the loft of the livery. "Colleen is sure a pretty girl."

"Go to sleep, Jeff. She isn't the only fish in the ocean. You'll feel better in the morning."

"I suppose so. Have you ever seen the ocean, Frank?"

"What?"

"The ocean. Have you ever seen it?"

"I've seen the Pacific Ocean a couple of times. It was beautiful."

Dog padded softly through the thick hay, and lay down between the two men and curled up. Frank reached out and petted the animal. Dog licked his hand and moved closer to him.

"She sure is a pretty girl," Jeff repeated.

Frank smiled in the darkness. "She'll be just as pretty in the morning, Jeff. After we get a good night's sleep."

Jeff didn't take the hint. "You've told me about your wife, Frank. Now tell me this, if you will..."

Frank waited. And waited. Finally he asked, "What it is, Jeff?"

"Was there ever another lady you cared for?"

"No."

"You've been in love just the one time?"

"I reckon so, Jeff. There have been other women, yes. But they were just passing interests."

"Ships that pass in the night."

"I beg your pardon?"

"Longfellow."

"Oh. Go to sleep, Jeff. Tomorrow is going to be a very busy day."

"Yes. Of course. We have to find us a place to live and I have to stake out some sort of claim, right?"

"That's right."

"I'll put Colleen out of my mind."

"I sure hope so. If you don't, it's going to be a damn long night."

Thirteen

Both men were awakened abruptly by the banging of a bass drum and blowing of a bugle.

"What in the hell!" Frank said, sitting straight up on the hay, throwing his blankets to one side, and grabbing for his pistol.

"Is it the end of the world?" Jeff asked.

"It's horrible!" a citizen shouted from just outside the livery.

"What is it?" another shouted.

"Paulette Tremaine's done got religion and shut down her house."

"Oh, no!"

"All the whores done quit too. They've all joined the church and the Temperance Movement."

"You don't mean it?"

"I do. It's all the fault of that buffalo-butted

woman from back East, that damned Martha Hornblower."

"Hornblower?"

"Something like that. It's all her fault. She's leadin' a torchlight parade down Main Street and there's gonna be a big meetin' right afterward."

"Martha Overhouser," Jeff said.

"The one and only," Frank said, lying back down and pulling the blankets over him.

"You don't want to go see?"

"Hell, no! Someone's liable to take a shot at Martha."

Jeff chuckled in the darkness of the loft.

"What's so funny?" Frank asked.

"If she was bent over, even I could hit her."

"She is mighty ample in the rear end, for a fact."

The drum-beating and horn-tooting became louder, and the reflection of dozens of torches could be seen through the open loft door.

"Whole bunch of ladies out there," Jeff said, crawling to the loft door and looking out. "And some men too."

"In the parade?"

"Yes."

"Local ministers, I bet."

"And there's Martha, leading the pack."

"Can you see Colleen?"

"Colleen? Why...she wouldn't be involved in something this silly."

"Don't bet on it."

"I think I'll go down and take a look."

"You go right ahead. Me and Dog will stay

here. You can tell me all about it in the morning."

"This is important, Frank." Jeff pulled on his boots.

"Not to me."

"Well, I'll try not to wake you when I get back."

"Have fun." Frank snuggled deeper into the hay, Dog moved closer to him, and they both went back to sleep.

When he woke early the next morning, Jeff had not returned. Frank dressed and got Dog down from the loft. The temperature was below freezing. Frank figured it was in the mid-twenties, but there was little wind, and that helped. Frank checked his watch: five o'clock.

"You stay here," Frank told Dog. Dog curled up in an empty stall. "I'll bring you back something to eat." Dog yawned and went back to sleep.

Frank walked over to a cafe that was just opening, and ordered a pot of coffee and breakfast. "Big doings here in town last night, huh?" he said to the waitress.

"Foolishness," she replied, filling his cup. "Marshal arrested about two dozen people... men and women."

"Did he now?" *And I'll bet Jeff was one of them.*

"Sure did. Amongst them was two preachers and that Overhouser woman and Paulette Tremaine. They're still in jail."

Frank ate his breakfast and drank his coffee, enjoying the warmth of the cafe and the good food. The cafe began to fill up and Frank stepped out into the cold. The lights were on at the marshal's office. Frank walked over and looked in the window. The marshal was seated at his desk, working on some papers. Frank tapped on the door and the marshal let him in.

"Morgan," the marshal said, surprise on his face as he waved Frank to a chair. "You have a problem?"

"No. But my young partner might. You have a Jeff Barton locked up?"

The marshal smiled. "Indeed I do."

"Damn! I figured as much. Disturbing the peace at the rally last night?"

"You got it. Most of those arrested have paid their fine and left. But several refused and I had no choice but to keep them locked down."

"Jeff Barton, Paulette Tremaine, and Martha Overhouser?"

"You got it square on the money, Morgan."

"And a young gal named Colleen?"

"Colleen O'Brian. How'd you know that?"

"Met Colleen and Martha Overhauser at a stage stop. Jeff's been riding with me. He's sort of smitten with Colleen. Paulette and Martha are old school friends from back East."

"Well, I'll be damned." The lawman grinned. "Say, you wouldn't like to be my deputy for a while, would you?"

"Not a chance, Marshal. Can I see Jeff?"

"Oh, sure. I was just about to take them some coffee. Help me tote it?"

"Be glad to."

The front door was pushed open and Conrad stepped in, all dressed to the nines, from his polished low-quarter shoes to his funny-looking hat. He was frowning, and his frown turned to a scowl when he looked at Frank. Two big bruisers stepped in right behind him. Conrad's bodyguards would probably tip the scales at about 250 pounds each, both of them looking as if they'd been carved out of solid oak.

Conrad did not speak to his father, just nodded and turned his attention to the marshal. "You have a young lady locked up, Marshal. A Miss Colleen O'Brian."

"Indeed I do."

"May I see her?"

"It's a little early, young man. Let me see if they're awake."

"Very well. We'll wait."

"Have a seat. Come on, Frank, you grab the cups, I'll tote the pot."

The marshal opened the door and Martha Overhouser hollered, "The accommodations in this prison are abysmal! Primitive, to say the least."

"Your mouth got you in here, lady," the marshal said. "Ten dollars will get you out."

"Never!" Martha roared. "It's a matter of principle."

"Suit yourself. How about some coffee, ladies?"

"I would like some, please," Jeff said, not meeting Frank's eyes.

"Me too," Paulette and Colleen said.

Frank passed out the tin cups, and the marshal filled them.

"I would like two sugars and a small bit of cream, please," Colleen said.

"Black or not at all, lady," the marshal told her.

"You are a very rude and crude person, Marshal Dickson!" Martha shouted.

"Your fine just went up to twenty dollars, Mrs. Overhouser," the marshal told her.

"Insensitive oaf!" Martha said.

"You want to keep trying for thirty dollars, lady?" Dickson asked her.

Martha sat down on the bunk and shut her mouth.

"Colleen!" Conrad snapped from the doorway. "I am very disappointed in you."

"Get your butt back out in the waiting area, boy!" Dickson told him.

"Don't you speak to me in such a manner, Marshal Dickson!" Conrad popped off.

"I'll speak to you in any damn way I feel like, boy. Now you get back into the waiting area and you stay there. Move, boy, or I'll put your ass in a cell."

Conrad opened his mouth, and Frank said, "Put a sock in it, son. Get out of here."

Conrad spun around and stalked out of the cell area, his back stiff as a poker.

"How much is Jeff's fine, Marshal?" Frank asked.

"Ten dollars."

"I have the money to pay my fine," Jeff said. "If I choose to do so. But I have done nothing wrong."

"Shut up," Frank told him. He looked at

114

Marshal Dickson. "What's he charged with?"

Dickson smiled. "There are about a dozen charges I could hang on him and Miss O'Brian. But if they'll pay just ten bucks each, I'll only charge them with creating a public nuisance."

"That's on the books?"

"It is now."

Frank laughed and handed the marshal twenty dollars. "That's for Jeff and the girl. The other two are on their own."

"Stand firm, Colleen!" Martha yelled. "Don't yield to pressures from a man."

"How about me?" Paulette asked from another cell.

"I ought to send you to the territorial prison, Paulette," Dickson told her. "You're long overdue in my book."

"Try it, you officious piss-ant!" Paulette challenged him. "I know the judge...in more ways than one."

Muttering under his breath about soiled doves in general and Paulette Tremaine in particular, Dickson opened the cell door and jerked Jeff out, then opened another door and hauled Colleen out. "The two of you get out of here. Move!"

"You and I will talk later on today, Colleen," Conrad said as the young lady walked into the waiting area of the marshal's office. "Your behavior last night was quite disgraceful. I'm very ashamed of you."

"I thought she was wonderful," Jeff said. "Standing up for her beliefs."

"Who asked you for your opinion?" Conrad popped right back, looking at Jeff the way a doctor might look at a germ. "You...you vagabond!"

"Boy does have a way with words, doesn't he?" the marshal said to Frank.

Before Frank could reply, Jeff took a step toward Conrad, his hands balled into fists. "You pompous little tyrant! You need a good thrashing!"

"Try it, you misbegotten sot!" Conrad came right back.

Frank was looking on, amused at the exchange. Conrad's bodyguards, however, were not amused. They moved closer to Conrad, ready to protect their boss.

"You boys stand easy," Frank told the pair of bruisers.

"Or you'll do what?" one asked.

"Put more holes in you than you can count," Frank replied, pushing back his coat and slipping the thong off the hammer of his .45.

"He's a craven killer," Conrad advised his bodyguards. "He means it."

"A craven killer?" Jeff said, looking first at Conrad, then at Frank. "That's a damn lie! He's no craven killer."

"Are you calling me a liar?" Conrad shouted. "You...worthless bum!"

"Yes, I'm calling you a liar," Jeff came right back. "And I'm also calling you an arrogant, two-bit, petty little spoiled brat. What do you think about that, Fancy Pants?"

"I've a good mind to give you a proper thrashing!" Conrad said.

"All by yourself, or with the help of your hired thugs?" Jeff asked.

"I ain't no thug," one of the bodyguards objected. "Where the hell you get off callin' me a thug?"

"Me neither," his partner said. "That's a damn insult I don't have to take."

"I don't need any help," Conrad said, removing his coat. "I boxed in school and I am quite skilled in the art of pugilism."

"What the hell does that mean?" Marshal Dickson asked Frank.

"Means he thinks he knows how to fight."

Jeff took off his coat and balled his hands into fists.

"Stop this!" Colleen said.

"Stay out of this, dear," Jeff told her.

"Dear?" Conrad shouted. "How dare you call my girl dear?"

"I'm quite flattered," Colleen said to Conrad. "And I am not your girl."

"You cheap little slut!" Conrad told her.

"That does it," Jeff said. He stepped in close to Conrad and popped the young man on the snoot.

The fight was on.

Fourteen

Conrad was knocked to the floor. "You 'oke my 'ose!" Conrad hollered, holding his busted beak.

"I'll break more than that!" Jeff yelled.

Conrad kicked out and his shoe caught Jeff on the knee. Jeff started cussing and went hobbling one-legged around the room, yelling and holding onto his aching knee.

Conrad got to his feet, his nose bloody. He set himself in his best prizefighter pose: left arm fully extended in front of him, right hand held close to his chest, both hands balled into fists.

"Is he going to fight or pose for a statue?" Marshal Dickson questioned.

"Damned if I know," Frank replied.

Jeff carefully tested his knee, found that it worked, and faced Conrad. "Now you get thrashed," he told the younger man.

Conrad's reply was to pop Jeff on the jaw. The blow staggered him back. Jeff recovered, and gave Conrad a left shot to the belly and a right fist to the side of the head.

The two then stood toe-to-toe for half a minute, slugging it out, each giving back as much as he got.

"Pretty damn good fight," Marshal Dickson said.

"Oh, stop this!" Colleen begged.

The men paid no attention to her.

"Time, time!" Conrad said.

"Time's butt," Jeff said, and knocked him to the floor.

"Foul, foul!" Conrad yelled.

"That ain't fair," one of the bodyguards said. "That was an uncalled-for blow."

"This ain't no prize ring, boys," Dickson said.

Conrad jumped to his shoes and popped Jeff on the nose.

"Ouch!" Jeff hollered, putting both hands to his nose. Conrad gave him a left and right to the belly.

"Give it to him, Mr. Browning!" a bodyguard yelled.

"I can't stand this!" Colleen screamed.

"You can leave, miss," the marshal told her.

Colleen looked at Frank. "Stop this!"

Frank shrugged. "They're fighting over you, Colleen, not me." Jeff hauled off and knocked Conrad through the office window. Conrad landed on his butt on the boardwalk.

Jeff crawled through the broken window after him.

"Whoever wins the fight gets to pay for that broken window," Marshal Dickson said.

"Sounds fair to me," Frank replied.

Conrad and Jeff were slugging it out on the boardwalk, Colleen was screaming, Martha and Paulette were hollering back in the cell area, and a crowd was gathering in the street to watch the fight in front of the marshal's office.

Frank and Marshal Dickson stepped outside to watch the fight, the bodyguards with them.

All in all, it was a typical day in the mining town of Durango.

Conrad and Jeff rolled off the boardwalk and into the muddy street, still cussing and flailing away at each other, but doing little damage.

"I think they've just about had it," Frank remarked.

" 'Pears that way to me," Dickson said.

Jeff and Conrad staggered to their feet and stood panting and glaring at one another.

"That's it, boys," Dickson said, stepping off the boardwalk and into the street. "Fight's over."

Conrad reared back and took a swing at Jeff. He ducked and the punch caught the marshal flush in the mouth. Dickson's feet flew out from under him and he landed on his butt in the mud.

The crowd cheered.

Conrad's feet slipped in the mud and he began flailing his arms, trying to keep his balance. He didn't make it. He fell heavily into Jeff and they went down together, landing with a big slopping sound in a mud puddle in front of a horse trough.

The crowd cheered and applauded.

"Good Lord!" Frank muttered.

"Get me out of here!" Conrad yelled.

"Somebody get this crazy crackpot off me!" Jeff yelled.

"Crazy crackpot!" Conrad yelled. "Why... you...you worthless hobo. You..."

He never got a chance to finish it. Jeff popped him on the nose. Again.

"Oww!" Conrad yelled. " 'Ou don't 'ight 'air. My 'ose is 'eally 'oken now!"

"Good," Jeff yelled. "I'll make sure." He hit Conrad again. On the nose.

Conrad hollered and jumped up, both hands holding his busted beak.

Frank decided it had gone far enough. He waded in and grabbed Conrad, slinging him into the arms of his bodyguards. "Hold on to him and don't turn him loose." He reached down and jerked Jeff to his boots. "It's over, damnit! Now calm down." He gave Jeff a shove that propelled him into the base of the horse trough. Jeff did a belly flop into the icy water.

He came up sputtering and hollering.

Frank looked at the bodyguards. "Get your boss out of here, right now." He hauled Jeff out of the horse trough and shoved him toward the barbershop. "Get over there and tell the barber to start heating up some hot water. I'll bring your clothes over."

"Who won the fight?" Jeff asked, shivering in the cold air.

"I'd call it a draw."

Frank paid for the broken window. Then he got Dog something to eat from a cafe and saddled his horse. He got Jeff some clean clothes and took them over to the bathhouse, and waited until Jeff had finished his bath and was dressed.

"Go on back to the livery and take care of Dog until I get back. Can you do that without getting into a brawl?"

"Yes, Frank."

"Good. I should be back by midafternoon, or sooner. Now go on."

"Where are you going?"

"To find us a place to stay."

"How's Conrad?"

"Probably madder than hell."

"How is Colleen?"

"I have no idea. Now go on back to the livery and, by God, stay there."

Frank headed out of town, but he had no plans to look for a place to stay. He had already found one that was owned by the marshal and paid several months' rent on the place.

He wanted to check out the country and do it alone. And he wanted to see if he might be followed.

As he rode, Frank smiled as he thought about the fight. Conrad was sure as hell no sissy-boy. He was a pretty good puncher and wasn't afraid to wade right in and mix it up. Now if the boy would just get rid of that damn silly hat.

Frank rode for several hours and could detect no signs of being followed. The Pine and Vanbergen gangs either did not yet know he was in the area, or didn't care. Probably they didn't know. But they would, he was certain of that. Both Ned and Vic wanted him dead.

Frank headed back to town, arriving at midafternoon. The weather had turned sour, the skies thick with low gray clouds that promised a blanket of snow before morning.

Jeff was in the loft of the livery, rolled up in his blankets, Dog snuggled up next to him in the hay. Frank shook him awake.

"I have us a place to live, Jeff. Let's get moved in. Rattle your hocks."

"I feel really terrible. I think I'm coming down with something."

"You probably are. Move."

The two-bedroom house Frank had rented was well built and furnished, with a small barn out back. Frank sent Jeff to the general store to buy bedding and a few pots and pans, a coffeepot, and a few basic supplies. Frank built a fire in the Franklin Stove and in the stove in the kitchen, then primed the pump in the kitchen and got it working.

Dog had carefully inspected each room in the house, and after circling the spot a dozen times, apparently had found himself a place to bed down in the small living room.

"We'll spend the winter here, boy," Frank told him. "I hope," he added.

"I broke your boy's nose and gave him a fat lip," Jeff announced, placing the supplies on the table in the kitchen.

Frank looked at Jeff's face. It was bruised and Jeff was sporting a shiner. "You both got marked. Did you see Colleen in town?"

"Yes. She found a job working for the local paper."

"As a reporter?"

"Sort of. She's quite thrilled about it. We're going to a social tomorrow evening."

"Oh?"

"Yes. Conrad apparently wants no more to do with her. I'm told he's sworn off women forever."

Frank chuckled. "That'll last for at least a day or two. Are you feeling better?"

"Yes. Much better. I just have a small head cold. But I'm very tired for some reason."

"Eat a good supper and then go to bed. I'll fix us some bacon and eggs."

"That sounds wonderful."

Long after Jeff had gone to bed and was sleeping soundly, Frank sat in the small living room, the lamp turned down low, drinking coffee, wondering what his next move should be. The fire of revenge that had burned in his belly for weeks after his cabin was destroyed and Dog was shot had become only a small smoldering. Going after Ned and Vic would not bring Vivian back, it would not rebuild his cabin, nor would it ease the days and nights of suffering that Dog had experienced.

So what the hell would be the point of long exhausting weeks on the trail, through the bitter cold and blowing snow, to gun down a pack of worthless men that the law would catch and hang sooner or later?

No point at all.

"Hell with it," Frank whispered to the shadowy room. "Durango is as good a place as any to hole up for the winter. I sure don't have to worry about money."

Dog padded over to him, and Frank petted the animal. "Maybe we can stay put here for a few months, boy. Would you like that?"

Dog whined and wagged his tail.

"It's settled then. We'll stay here for a while."

During the next several weeks, Jeff staked out a claim and actually began finding some decent color. Paulette Tremaine's soiled doves went back to work, doing what they did best...freelancing in the town's many saloons.

Paulette and Martha founded the Durango Christian Temperance and Women's Rights League, and proceeded to make a nuisance of themselves.

Jeff and Colleen were seeing each other on a regular basis, and love appeared to be in full bloom. Frank figured they'd get hitched up come spring.

Conrad kept pretty much to himself, and when he and Frank would see each other, the young man chose not to acknowledge his presence. Frank didn't push the issue. Conrad would come around someday, or he wouldn't. There wasn't a damn thing Frank could do about it, one way or the other.

Christmas and New Year's came and went and the weather turned lousy, with lots of snow and bitterly cold temperatures. Frank kept busy chopping wood and hauling it back to town with a wagon and team rented from the livery.

Dog stayed inside mostly and put on weight.

February drifted into March, and the weather began to moderate.

"We hit the trail come spring, boy," Frank told him. "You're going to lose some of that fat."

Dog wagged his tail and looked at his empty food bowl.

"Later," Frank told him. "You're getting fat! Why don't you go catch a rabbit?"

Dog looked at him as though he had lost his mind, and wandered over to his bed for a nap.

"Too quiet for the past couple of months," Frank muttered as he fixed a pot of coffee. "Something real bad is fixin' to happen. I can feel it. I hope I'm wrong, but I don't think I am."

Frank answered a knock on the front door, and looked into the worried face of Marshal Dickson. He waved him inside. "I was just thinking that it was too damn quiet and that something was due to happen. I reckon it has."

"It has, Frank. Conrad Browning's been kidnapped."

Fifteen

Conrad had stepped out for lunch and never returned. The two bodyguards that accompanied him were found in a shed behind the cafe. Their throats had been cut. The other two bodyguards had disappeared without a trace. A bloodstained note had been found, pinned to the chest of one of the dead bodyguards with a knife. The note demanded a million dollars for Conrad's safe return. If the money was not paid, the young man would die.

Frank stared for a moment in disbelief at the marshal. "A million dollars?"

"That's what the note said."

"I can't even imagine a million dollars!"

"I can't either. When it gets past a couple of thousand, my brain gets boggled."

"Who signed the note?"

Dickson handed the bloodstained note to Frank. It was unsigned. "This is it?" Frank asked.

"That's it. Now you know as much as I do."

"No instructions."

"None."

Frank handed the note back to the marshal. "The two missing bodyguards?"

"For sure they had something to do with it. But there were at least half a dozen boot prints back of the cafe and bloody boot prints in the shed."

"Pine and Vanbergen."

"That's my thinkin'."

"Do you know their hideout, Marshal?"

Dickson shook his head. "No. I honest to God do not. I've talked with other lawmen who say it changes from time to time. From the canyon country badlands west of here to the mountains north of here. Take your pick."

"Have you ever chased them?"

Again, Dickson shook his head. "They've never committed a crime in this town. At least not to my knowledge. And I don't know a damn thing about the badlands."

"Do me a favor?"

"Sure. Name it."

"Find Jeff and tell him to look after Dog. I'm going to gear up and try to pick up their trail."

"If he can't look after him, I promise you I will. I'll take good care of him. You have my word. I like that mutt."

Frank packed quickly but carefully and saddled up, then rigged the packsaddle on his packhorse. Then he filled up Dog's water bowl and food dish.

"Now you be good and mind people, you hear me?" he told Dog.

Dog looked up from his food dish and wagged his tail, then resumed his dining.

Frank rode into town and provisioned up. While the shopkeeper was filling his order, Frank checked the tracks in back of the cafe, and found a couple of horseshoe prints that were very distinctive. One shoe had a distinctive marking, and one of the horses had an odd way of putting down his right front hoof.

"Now I can follow you to hell, boys," he muttered. He was back in the saddle in half an hour, heading out of town. The tracks led straight north.

"Better than heading down into Ute country," Frank said aloud, although there was not much fight left in the Utes now.

There was still snow on the ground in many places, and that made tracking a lot easier.

The kidnappers were following an old Indian trail that Frank felt sure had originally been a game trail. The stage road was a few miles to Frank's east, but those few miles were over some rugged and inhospitable terrain. The day was bright with sunshine and the temperature, Frank thought, was probably in the mid-forty range. The snow was melting quickly in the lower elevations. The nights were still well below freezing, usually in the mid-twenties.

The kidnappers had several hours' jump on Frank, and Frank was pretty sure the outlaws would have fresh horses hidden along the way. There was no way he could catch up to them without killing his horses, something he had no intention of doing.

A half day's hard ride north of Durango, the trail abruptly turned west. Frank rested his horses while he inspected the trail sign on foot. After casting around for several minutes, he discovered that half of the outlaws had continued on north, the other half west.

"Damn!" Frank muttered.

He had no way of knowing which group was holding his son captive.

Either way was rough country, but north was slightly worse and colder.

"West." Frank made up his mind. "And I hope I'm right."

Frank spent an uncomfortable night on the trail, the first of what would turn out to be many, and was back dogging the outlaws at first light. During the cold night, Frank awakened often to add wood to the small fire and to think. He didn't believe his son was kidnapped solely for ransom...a million dollars was totally unrealistic. He believed, in part, that Conrad had been taken to pull Frank out of Durango. Ned Pine and Victor Vanbergen had grabbed Conrad knowing Frank would follow and they could kill him, or try to kill him.

But if that was the case, then why did the trail suddenly split?

Just maybe, Frank thought, the bodyguards who were in cahoots with the Pine and Vanbergen gangs had been paid off and sent on their way.

Lingering over coffee at his nooning, Frank decided that was it.

He knew that Pine and Vanbergen hated him with an unbridled passion; he had been told that both had sworn to kill him many times. He suspected they had killed Vivian, not just for the money Dutton had surely paid them, but to get at him.

"Sorry bastards," Frank muttered, pouring another cup of coffee and munching on hard crackers. *Well,* he thought, *if you've done this to get me on your trail, boys, you've damn sure succeeded.*

Frank's horses suddenly became alert, their heads coming up, ears pricked in attention. A twig popped faintly in the timber. Frank dropped his coffee cup and threw himself to one side just as gunfire ripped the cold stillness.

Rifle in hand, he rolled toward a fallen log and hunkered down behind the small protection.

One man, Frank thought, *off to my left in that thicket of brush.*

Frank held his fire, wanting the sniper to expose himself. He waited, but no more shots came.

A few minutes ticked past. Frank rolled from behind the protection of the log and into brush. No shots followed him. He slipped deeper into the brush and then into the timber, carefully working his way toward the thicket. He heard a slight noise and paused, listening intently. The faint sounds of a horse moving away reached him. Frank ran toward the fading sound, hoping to get in at least one shot. He was too late. The unknown sniper had gotten away. He knelt down and inspected the hoof tracks. He could not tell if they were part of the group that had left the tracks behind the cafe in town, and it was still a mystery as to whether or not he was following the group that had his son.

But he now suspected more than ever that he was.

Frank mounted up and rode on. Before he had gone a mile, he came across the fresh tracks of his ambusher. The man had swung back onto the trail and was traveling as fast as he could over the rough terrain.

Frank reined up. He had to give this situation some thought. The ambusher knew he was following, and also knew he wasn't going to stop following. That made Frank a very conspicuous target. What to do about that? He couldn't leave the trail, for if he did that it might take him hours or days to pick it up, or he might never pick it up.

Frank shucked his rifle out of the saddle scabbard and started on, his rifle held in one hand, across the saddle horn.

He would ride a few hundred yards, then rein up and carefully check out all that was in front of him. It slowed him down some, but was helping to keep him alive.

He moved on another half a mile, he reckoned, and abruptly stopped when he saw where the sniper had reined up and sat his horse for a time. Frank carefully scanned the terrain in front of him, his gaze always returning to one spot about five hundred yards in front of him and slightly to his right.

"Right there is where I'd choose for an ambush," he muttered. "Perfect cover and elevation. And I'll bet that's where the shooter is."

Frank stepped his horse off the trail and into deeper timber. He ground-reined both animals and took off his spurs. Then he set out on foot, swinging wide so he could come up behind the ambusher...he hoped.

As he drew ever closer, Frank caught the faint odor of tobacco. The man had built him a smoke while waiting, probably to try to steady his nerves for the kill.

Frank was much more cautious now, for while he knew approximately where the shooter was, he wasn't sure of the exact spot. He could be anywhere along that ridge, in the brush and timber. And from the sound of the rifle, he definitely wasn't shooting a .44 or a .44-.40. Probably one of those fancy new bolt-action rifles with maybe one of those high-powered telescope things on it. That type of rifle would have a much more accurate range to it than Frank's .44-.40. Definitely something to take into consideration.

Shortly after he swung in behind the ridge and started working his way up, Frank caught a flash of color, a color that was out of place in the brush and timber.

"There you are," Frank muttered.

Frank had a shot, but chose not to take it. He wanted the ambusher alive, if possible, to answer some questions.

Frank began slowly and furtively working his way up the ridge, utilizing every bit of cover. The ambusher came into clear view, and never looked around to check behind him.

When Frank was about twenty-five yards behind the man, with a clear shot if the fellow spun around and tried to shoot, Frank called, "Don't move, partner. Don't do anything stupid or you're dead."

The man froze in place. "Morgan?"

"That's right."

"Damn! Are you part Injun?"

"No. Just a man that's managed to stay alive by being real careful."

"I believe it."

"Lay the rifle down slow."

The man carefully laid his expensive-looking rifle with a telescope sight on it on the ground.

"Stand up and turn around," Frank told him. "And do it real careful. No sudden moves."

The ambusher stood up slowly. Without turning around, he asked, "Are you going to kill me, Morgan?"

"Not unless I have to."

"I don't believe you."

"Your choice. Live or die, it's all up to you."

The man stood with his back to Frank, his hands at his side. He refused to turn around.

"You're putting me on the spot, fellow," Frank said, "and you're playing a dangerous game."

The ambusher laughed. "What difference does it make? It's the only game in town."

"For a fact."

"I hear you're a fast gun, Morgan."

"Fast doesn't have anything to do with this situation. I've got a rifle pointed square at you."

"Well, now. If that's the case, I reckon that's true. I got me an idee: You wouldn't want to put that rifle down and let's you and me go head-to-head at it, would you, Morgan? Just see who's the fastest?"

"Why should I? I got nothing to prove, partner."

"Don't interest you at all, huh, Morgan?"

"Not in the least."

"Pity. Since I think you've slowed down. Man gets to be your age, he loses a lot. Includin' his nerve."

Frank smiled. "I know what you're trying to do but it won't work, partner."

"You're a cool one, Morgan. But I think I have to try you anyway."

"Then that makes you a fool."

"Won't be the first time."

"It'll be the last."

"Maybe."

The ambusher spun around, snaking his pistol from leather.

Sixteen

Frank's bullet hit the ambusher in the shoulder and sat him down on the cold ground.

"Damn!" the man said.

"That was a really stupid move, partner," Frank told him.

"I reckon so." He slowly lifted his six-gun. Frank took careful aim with his rifle and put a bullet into the man's right arm. The pistol dropped from his fingers.

"You want to try for another bullet or some conversation?" Frank asked.

"How about a doctor?"

"Can't help you there."

"My shoulder's on fire."

"Get used to it."

"You tryin' to tell me I'm headin' for the hell-fires?"

"Only two people can answer that, partner: you and God."

"I don't believe in none of that crap."

"Your option."

The ambusher groaned and stretched out on the ground.

Frank walked the distance between them and squatted down a few yards from the man. "You're not going to make it, partner."

"I know that, you son of a bitch!"

"You have a name?"

"Don't everybody?"

Frank waited.

"Charles Bowers," the ambusher finally said.

"Any kin?"

"No."

"Where's your horse? I'll turn him loose."

Charles cut his eyes. "Over yonder a ways. He's a good one. You ought to take him with you and sell him."

"Only if you have a bill of sale."

Charles smiled.

"That's what I figured. Where'd you steal him?"

"Didn't. The gang did somewheres. I don't rightly know where."

"Pine and Vanbergen gangs?"

"Yeah."

"What is this million-dollar crap in return for Conrad Browning?"

"To get you to follow us and kill you."

"And then what happens to Conrad?"

"He gets a bullet."

"So Pine and Vanbergen never planned on collecting any ransom money?"

"Not a dime."

"Where are they taking the boy?"

"West. Into the badlands."

"Into Ute country?"

"No. Just north of there."

"So I'm on the right track? Following the right bunch?"

"Yeah. Why lie about it now?"

"How much of what you're telling me is the truth?"

Charles laughed. "You figger it out, Drifter."

"To hell with you then. Die alone." Frank stood up and turned away.

"Where are you goin'?"

"Leaving."

"You gonna just ride off and leave me here for the critters to eat on?"

"That's about it."

"That ain't decent!"

"Neither are you."

"All right, all right!"

"All right what?"

"Sit back down. I'll tell you everything I know."

Seventeen

"You're a sneaky bastard, Morgan," Charles Bowers said, lying in a patch of bloody snow, his shoulder leaking crimson onto the snowfall. "Nobody ever snuck up on me like that before."

"There's first times for everything. Tell me where they took my boy and who has him. The trail split a few miles back and I need to know what tracks to follow. Don't lie to me or I'll finish you off right here. A bullet in the right place will send you to eternity. Where the hell are they taking my son?"

"Ned and his bunch have got him."

"Where's Victor Vanbergen?"

"They turned toward the river, to throw off any pursuit if you or some posse from Durango was getting too close. Ned's being real careful about this, and so is Vanbergen. They know about your old reputation."

"Conrad's with Pine?"

"Yeah. Sam and Buster and Josh too. Mack and Curtis are ridin' rear guard. Arnie and Scott rode on ahead to get the cabin ready. They figured you'd be behind them all the way, once you picked up their trail, Hell they're expecting you to show up."

"The cabin? What cabin?"

"It's an old hideout. Sits beside Stump Creek at the edge of the badlands. Way back in a box canyon. Ned's gonna send somebody back to Durango to tell you where the ransom money is supposed to be dropped off."

"Ned Pine's gotta be crazy. He knows I don't have that kind of money. Hell, all I'm gonna do is kill him and every one of his side-kicks."

Charles winced when the pain in his shoulder worsened. "It ain't gonna be as easy as you make it sound. They don't figure you've got big money. All Ned and Victor aim to do is kill you when you show up. They've got grudges against you from way back, and they won't rest easy 'til you're dead. Like I told you, it ain't gonna be easy gettin' close to 'em. They're gonna be ready for you."

"Depends," Frank said, squatting near Bowers.

"Depends on what?"

Frank chuckled mirthlessly. "On how mad I am when I get to that cabin."

"There's too many of 'em, Morgan. One of them will get you before you reach the kid. Ned Pine's about as good with a gun as any man I ever saw. He's liable to kill you himself, if the others don't beforehand."

"I wish him all the luck," Frank said. "I've been trying to quit the gunfighter's trade for several years. Then some bastard comes along like Ned Pine, or Vick Vanbergen, and they won't let it rest. But I can promise you one thing." Frank stared off at graying skies holding a promise of evening snow, a winter squall headed into the mountains.

"What's that, Morgan?"

Frank glared down at Bowers. "I'll kill every last one of them. I been getting some practice lately, and I can damn sure take down Ned Pine and his boys. One at a time, maybe, but I'll damn sure do it. Vanbergen don't worry me at all. He's yellow. He won't face me with a gun."

"Everybody says The Drifter is past his

prime, Morgan. I've heard it for years. You got too old to make it in this profession and folks know it."

"Maybe I am too old. Ned Pine and his owlhoots are about to test me, and then we'll see if old age has caught up to me. We'll know when this business is finished. It depends on who walks away."

"You damn sure don't act scared," Bowers hissed, clenching his teeth when more pain shot from his shoulder. "Ned claims you ain't got the nerve you used to have, back when you made a name for yourself. Hell, that was more 'n twenty years ago, according to Ned."

Frank chuckled again. "I ain't scared. Never met a man I was afraid of...leastways not yet."

"You gonna leave me here to die?" Bowers asked.

"Nope. I'm gonna take your guns and put you on that stolen stud. I'll tie your bandanna around your shoulder so you don't lose too much blood. It'll be up to you to find your way out of these mountains and canyons. I'm giving you a fifty-fifty chance to make it out of here alive. It's better odds than I aimed to give you."

"But I'm hurtin' real bad. I don't know if I can sit a saddle."

Frank shrugged, standing up with the ambusher's rifle cradled in his arm. "Better'n being dead, son. I'll fetch your horse and help you into the saddle."

"But Durango's fifty miles from here, across rough country to boot."

Frank halted on his way into the trees. "I can put you out of your misery now, if that's what you'd prefer. A slug right between the eyes and you won't feel a damn thing. You'll just go to sleep."

"You'd murder a man in cold blood?"

"Wasn't that what you were tryin' to do to me?"

Bowers laid his head back against a rotted tree trunk. "I reckon I'm obliged for what you're gonna do... I just ain't all that sure I'm gonna make it to town."

"Life don't have many guarantees, Bowers," Frank said. "You got one chance to make it. Stay in your saddle and aim for Durango. Otherwise, you're gonna be buzzard food. Hold on real tight to that saddle horn and if you know how to pray, you might try a little of that too."

He brought the bay stud back to the clearing. Bowers lay with his head on the rotten log, groaning softly, his shoulder surrounded by red snow.

"Sit up, Bowers," Frank demanded. "I'm gonna tied a bandanna around your shoulder."

"Jesus, my shoulder hurts," Bowers complained. "I don't think I can make it plumb to Durango."

"Suit yourself," Frank said. "You can lie here and bleed to death, or you can sit that horse and test your luck riding out of these mountains."

"You're cold-blooded, Morgan."

"I'm supposed to stop looking for my son long enough to help a no-good son of a bitch who was trying to ambush me?" he asked, his face turning hard. "You'd have left me for dead if you'd gotten off the first shot. Don't preach me any sermons about what a man's supposed to do."

"I ain't gonna make it," Bowers whimpered. "I've lost too much blood already."

"Then just lie there and go to sleep," Frank said. "It won't take too long. First, you'll get real cold. The chills will set in. Then you won't be able to keep your eyes open. In an hour or two, you'll doze off. That'll be about all you can remember."

"Damn, Morgan. You could take me to the closest doctor if you wanted."

"I don't have the inclination, Bowers. You and the man you work for have taken my son. He's eighteen years old. You want me to cough up a big ransom, more money than there is in the whole territory of Colorado, only you know I can't pay it. Ned Pine and the rest of you figured you'd lure me into a death trap, only I've got news for Ned. A death trap works two ways. The man who lays it can get killed just as easy as the bait he's tryin' to lure into it. Pine and Vanbergen are about to find out how it works."

"Help me on that horse, Morgan."

"I said I would. I'll tie a rag around your wound so the hole in you won't leak so bad."

"You got any whiskey?"

"Sure do. A pint of good Kentucky sour mash, only I ain't gonna waste any of it on you. It's gonna get cold tonight. I figure it's gonna snow. The whiskey I've got is gonna help me stay warm. I don't give a damn if you get froze stiff before you get back to Durango."

"You ain't got no feelings, Morgan."

"Not for trash like you. Nothing on earth worse than a damn bushwhacker."

"It's what Ned told me to do."

"Then ask Ned or Victor for some of their whiskey. Mine is staying in my saddlebags."

"I ain't gonna make it plumb to Durango," Charles said again as he tried to sit up.

"I'll notify your next of kin that you tried as hard as you could," Frank said, pulling off Bowers's bandanna. "Now sit up straight and pull off your coat so I can tie this around that shoulder as tight as I can."

"It damn sure hurts," Bowers said, sliding his mackinaw off his damaged arm.

"A shame," Frank told him. "Seems like they ought to make a slug that don't cause any pain when it takes a rotten bushwhacker down. No sense in hurting a dirty back-shooter any more than it's absolutely necessary."

Frank hoisted Charles Bowers into the saddle, his mackinaw covering the bandage he had made for his shoulder wound. As the sun lowered in the west, spits of snow began to fall.

"Tell me where I find Stump Creek," Frank said. "Then direct me to the cabin."

"Stump Creek is due west...maybe ten more miles across this bunch of ravines. When you get to the first creek, you swing north. Stump Creek winds right up in that canyon where the cabin is hid."

"If there isn't any cabin or any creek, I'm gonna come looking for you," Frank warned.

"It's there. They're both there. When you get to the canyon they'll have a guard or two posted high on them rock walls on either side. Watch your ass."

"I always do. Now you'd best head for Durango. It'll take you all night to make the ride."

"It's snowin', Morgan. How about just one sip of the sour mash?"

"I already told you... I don't waste good whiskey on back-shooters. Besides, you've got a leak in your arm. Why let good whiskey spill out on the ground?"

"You're a bastard, Morgan."

"Maybe so. But I'm still alive. Unless you get to Durango by sunrise, the same can't be said for you. Keep that horse aimed southeast. Don't let go of the saddle horn. If you're as tough as you say you are, you'll make it."

"And if I don't? What if I freeze to death?"

"You'll make a good meal for the coyotes and wolves. Now get riding."

"How 'bout giving me back my rifle. I may need it if the wolves get too close. They can smell blood."

"No deal. You used it to take a shot at me. What's to keep you from trying it again?"

"You've got my word, Morgan. All I'm trying to do is stay alive."

"Then you'll have to do it without a gun. Heel that horse southeast."

"I wish I'd have killed you, Drifter."

Frank gave him a one-sided grin. "Plenty of men have wished the same thing. The trouble is, so far, wishing just hasn't gotten it done."

Bowers drummed his heels into the bay stallion's sides as more snow pelted down on the clearing.

Frank watched Bowers ride out of sight into the trees. "He'll make it," Frank muttered, heading for his saddle horse and packhorse with Bowers's rifle in the crook of his arm.

He needed to keep moving until dark, if the weather allowed, until he found Stump Creek. During the night he would give the canyon and the cabin an examination, making plans for the way he would make his approach tomorrow morning.

Snow began to fall in windblown sheets as he mounted his horse and wound the lead rope on his packhorse around his saddle horn.

He turned northwest. "I'm coming, Pine," he said, tilting his hat brim to block the snow. "Conrad damn sure better be in good shape when I get there."

It had been years since Frank Morgan went on the prowl to kill a man, or several of them. He'd tried to put his killing days behind him.

"Some folks just won't let it alone...won't let it rest," he told himself.

He had no doubts that he could kill Ned Pine,

145

or Victor Vanbergen, and their gangs. It would take some time to get it done carefully.

The soft patter of snowflakes drummed on his hat brim and coat. He thought about Conrad, hoping the boy was okay. A kid his age had no way to prepare for the likes of Pine and Vanbergen in these more modern times. But back when Frank was a boy, the country was full of them.

"I'm on my way, son," he whispered, as a wall of white fell in front of him. "Just hang on until I get there. I promise I'll make those bastards pay for what they've done to you."

Eighteen

Frank's shoulders were hunched into the wind, the collar of his mackinaw turned up, the brim of his hat pulled down against a building wall of snow.

"Just my luck," he muttered, guiding his horse up a snowy ridge, leading his packhorse. "Even the weather's turned against me."

But with Conrad's life on the line, no amount of hardship would turn him aside. The boy couldn't take care of himself against a gang of white-trash gunslingers. But Frank still had it in him to fill an outlaw's body with lead... old age hadn't robbed him of the skill. Or the speed.

All that mattered now was finding Conrad,

and getting him away from Ned Pine and his shootists. Conrad would be no match for them.

"Hell, he's only eighteen," Frank said into the wind as more snow pelted him.

His first objective was to find a stream called Stump Creek and then ride north along its banks. If Bowers hadn't been telling him the truth about the outlaw gang's hideout, he would track him down and kill him...if the weather and a shoulder wound didn't get Bowers first before he got to Durango.

Crossing the ridge, Frank spotted an unexpected sight, an old mountain man leading a mule.

"Seems harmless enough. Most likely an old trapper or a grizzly hunter."

Most of the old-time mountain men were gone now. Times had changed.

To be on the safe side, Frank opened his coat so he could reach for his Colt Peacemaker. His Winchester was booted to his saddle, just in case a fight started at longer range, although he didn't expect any such thing. The old man in deerskins was minding his own business, leading his mule west into the storm with his head lowered.

The mountain man wearing the coonskin cap heard Frank's horses coming down the ridge. He stopped and watched Frank ride toward him, the mountain man's right hand near a belted pistol at his waist. He was out in the open, dozens of yards from any cover. He crouched a little, like he was ready for action.

"No need to pull that gun, stranger!" Frank called. "I mean you no harm."

The gray-bearded man grinned. "Hell of a thing, to be caught out in this squall. Don't see many travelers in these parts, mister."

"The name's Frank Morgan. I'm looking for Stump Creek, and a cabin north of here in a box canyon."

The mountain man scowled. "What in tarnation would you want with the old robbers' roost? Are you on the dodge from the law someplace?"

"Nope...leastways not around here. A gang of cutthroats led by a jasper named Ned Pine has taken my eighteen-year-old son as hostage. I aim to get my boy back."

"Ol' Ned Pine," the trapper said, his mule loaded with game traps and cured beaver skins. "I'd be real careful if I was you. Pine is a killer. So are the boys who run with him. They ain't no good, not a one of 'em."

"Like I said, my son is their prisoner. I'm gonna kill every last one of them if I have to. I need directions to that creek, and the cabin."

The mountain man cocked his head. "Ain't one man tough enough to get that job done, Morgan. I know all about Pine and his hoodlums. They'll kill a man for sneezin' if he gets too close to 'em. Maybe you oughta rethink what you're plannin' to do before it gets you killed. There could be as many as a dozen of 'em."

Frank nodded. "I'll think on it long and hard, mister, but I'd be obliged if you'd point me in the direction of Stump Creek and that hideout."

"Keep movin' northwest. You'll hit the creek in about ten miles. Turn due north and follow the creek into the canyon where Stump Creek has its headwaters."

"I'm grateful. Names don't mean all that much out here, but you can give me your handle if you're so inclined."

"Tin Pan is what I go by. Spent years pannin' these streams lookin' for color. Never found so much as a single nugget, but there's plenty of beaver pelts to be had."

"Appreciate the information, Tin Pan. I won't make it to the creek until it's nearly dark. If you're of a mind to share a little coffee and fatback with a stranger, you can look for my fire."

"Might just do that, Morgan. It gets a mite lonely out on these slopes. Besides, I'm plumb out of coffee. Been out for near a month now. But I've got a wild turkey hen we can spit on them flames tonight. Turkey an' fatback sounds mighty good, if it comes with coffee."

"You'll be welcome at my fire, Tin Pan. I'm headed west and north until I hit the creek. I'll have a pot of coffee on by the time you get there leading that mule."

"I can cover more ground than most folks figure. A mule has got more gumption than a horse when the weather gets bad. I'll be there...pretty close behind you, unless I get a shot at a good fat deer. It'll take me half an hour to gut him and skin him proper."

Tin Pan had a Sharps booted to the pack-saddle on his mule. There was something confident about the way the old man carried himself.

"Venison goes good with coffee," Frank said. He gazed into the snowstorm. "The only thing I've got to be careful about is having Ned Pine or a member of his gang spot my campfire. I may have to find a spot sheltered by trees to throw up my canvas lean-to. I don't want them to know I'm coming."

Tin Pan shook his head. "Not in this snow. The cabin you talked about is miles up the creek anyhow. Only a damn fool would be out in a storm like this. I reckon that makes both of us damn fools, don't it?"

Frank chuckled. "Hard to argue against it. I'll find that creek and get a fire and coffee going. It's gonna be pitch dark in an hour or two. I need to find the right spot to hide my horses and gear from prying eyes."

"You won't have no problems tonight, Morgan," Tin Pan said. "But if it stops snowin' before sunrise, you'll have more than a passel of troubles when the sun comes up. A man on a horse sticks out like a sore thumb in this country after it snows, if the sun is shinin'. That's when you'll have to be mighty damn careful."

"See you in a couple of hours," Frank said, urging his horse forward. "Just thinking about a cup of hot coffee and a frying pan full of fatback has got my belly grumbling."

"I'll be there," the mountain man assured him. "Sure hope you got a lump of sugar to go with that coffee."

"A bag full of brown sugar," Frank said over his shoulder as he rode down the ridge.

"Damn if I ain't got the luck today," Tin Pan cried as Frank rode out of sight into a stand of pines at the bottom of a steep slope.

Frank rode directly into the snowfall, his hands and face numbed by the cold. The outlaws' trail would be gone in an hour or less, with so much snow falling. He'd have to rely on the information Bowers and the mountain man gave him.

His horses were tied in a pine grove. Frank huddled over a small fire, begging it to life by blowing on what little dry tinder he could find.

Stump Creek lay before him, a name he supposed the stream had earned due to the work by a beaver colony. All up and down the creek's banks, stumps from gnawed-down trees dotted the open spots.

The clear creek still flowed, with only a thin layer of ice on it. It was easy to break through to get enough water to fill his coffeepot.

He poured a handful of scorched coffee beans into the pot and set it beside the building flames. Surrounding the fire pit with a few flat stones, he had cooking surfaces on which he could place his skillet full of fatback.

If Tin Pan found his camp, it would be

easy enough to rig a spit out of green pine limbs and skewer hunks of turkey onto sticks above the fire. Just thinking about a good meal made him hurry.

In a matter of minutes the sweet aroma of boiling coffee filled the clearing in the pines. Frank warmed his hands over the flames, letting his thoughts drift back to Conrad, and Ned Pine's gunslicks.

"I swear I'm gonna kill 'em," he said to himself. "They better not have done any harm to my boy or I'll make 'em die slow."

His saddle horse raised its head, looking east with its ears pricked forward.

"That'll be the old mountain man," Frank said, standing up to walk to the edge of the pine grove. An experienced mountain man Tin Pan's age would be able to follow the scent of his fire from miles away.

Frank looked up at the darkening sky. Swirls of snowflakes fell on the pine limbs around him.

"I'll need to rig my lean-to," he mumbled. "No telling how much it'll snow tonight.

"Hello, the fire!" a distant voice shouted.

"Come on in!" Frank replied. "Coffee's damn near done boiling!"

"I smelt it half an hour ago, Morgan!"

He saw the shape of Tin Pan leading his mule down to the creek through a veil of snow. It would be good to have a bit of company tonight. He was sure the old man had a sackful of stories about these mountains. Maybe even some information about the hideout where Ned Pine was holding Conrad.

Frank buttoned his coat and turned up the collar; then he picked up more dead pine limbs to add to the fire. But even as the prospects of good company and a warm camp lay foremost in his mind he couldn't shake the memory of Conrad and the outlaw bastards who held him prisoner.

"Damn, that's mighty good," Tin Pan said, palming a tin cup of coffee for its warmth, with two lumps of brown sugar to sweeten it.

"I've got plenty," Frank told him. "I provisioned myself at Durango."

Tin Pan's wrinkled face looked older in light from the flames. "I been thinkin'," he said. Then he fell silent for a time.

"About what?" Frank asked.

"Ned Pine. Your boy. That hideout up in the canyon where you said they was hidin'."

"What about it?"

"It's mighty hard to get into that canyon without bein' seen, unless you know the old Ute trail."

"The Utes cleared out of this country years ago, after the army got after them," Frank recalled.

"That still don't keep a man from knowin' the back way into that canyon," Tin Pan said.

"There's a back way?"

Tin Pan nodded. "An old game trail. When these mountains were full of buffalo, the herds used it to come down to water in winter."

"Can you tell me how to find it?"

Tin Pan shook his head. "I'd have to show it to you. It's steep. A man who don't know it's there will ride right past it without seein' a thing."

Frank sipped scalding coffee, seated on his saddle blanket near the fire. "I don't suppose you'd have time to show me where it was."

"I might. You seem like a decent feller, and you've sure got your hands full, trying to take on Ned Pine and his bunch of raiders."

"I could pay you a little something for your time," Frank said.

Tin Pan hoisted his cup of coffee. "This here cup of mud will be enough."

"Then you'll show me that trail?"

"Come sunrise, I'll take you up to the top of that canyon. I've got some traps I need to set anyhow."

"I'd be real grateful. My boy is only eighteen. He won't stand a chance against Pine and his ruffians."

"Don't get me wrong, Morgan. I ain't gonna help you fight that crowd. But I'll show you the back way down to the floor of the canyon. They won't be expectin' you to slip up on 'em from behind."

"I've got an extra pound of coffee beans. It's yours if you'll show me the trail."

"You just made yourself a trade, Mr. Morgan. A pound of coffee beans will last me a month."

"It's done, Tin Pan," Frank said, feeling better about things now. "I'm gonna pitch my lean-to while the fatback is cooking."

Tin Pan grinned. "I'll cut some green sticks

for the hen I shot this morning. A man can't hardly ask for more'n turkey and fatback, along with sweet coffee."

Nineteen

Sam signaled a halt. "Yonder's a fire. Maybe it's Charlie on his way back to the cabin after he ambushed that bastard Frank Morgan."

"Who the hell else would be out here?" Tony asked as he peered into the snow.

Buster jerked his pistol free, his back to the heavy snowfall. "We gotta be sure, boys," he said to Sam and Tony. "I've heard stories about Morgan. He ain't no tinhorn, even if he is gettin' on in years. Let's ride up real careful, just to be on the safe side."

"You worry too much," Tony said. "Charlie Bowers is as good as they come when a man needs killin'. That's how come Ned sent him back to do the job. Charlie don't miss. He's as good as they get for a bushwhackin' job."

"All the same," Sam said, drawing his own Colt .44, "we'll ride up careful. No sense in takin' any chances. It could even be some deer hunter or a traveler. But it pays to be cautious with Morgan followin' your tracks."

"Remember what Ned told us," Tony warned. "Frank Morgan is a killer, a professional shootist from way back. He may still have a lot of caution in him."

"Ned's too worried about Morgan," Sam declared. "Besides, he's just one man and there's three of us. You ain't giving Charlie enough credit. My money says he planted Morgan in a shallow grave by now."

"We've got the wind at our backs," Tony said. "Let's ride around and come at him upwind, whoever the hell he is."

"Sounds like a good idea," Sam agreed. "If it's Charlie camped down by that creek, we'll recognize him. If it ain't, if it's Morgan, we start shootin' until that sumbitch is dead."

"Morgan's already dead," Sam said. "The only thing worryin' Ned is why Bowers didn't come back to the cabin by dark. Charlie knows his way around these mountains. Maybe all that happened was his stud went lame."

"I don't like the looks of this, Sam," Tony said, squirming in his saddle. "There's something about this that don't feel quite right."

"You're a natural-born worrier, Tony," Sam said. "If it is Frank Morgan down there by that fire, the three of us will kill him."

The gunslicks rode south into the snowy night with guns drawn.

Larger flakes of snow had begun to fall, and the howl of the squall winds echoed through the treetops around them.

"Clarence Rushing is my full name," Tin Pan said, pouring himself another cup of coffee. "I've been up in these mountains so long that

156

the other gold-panners hung the Tin Pan handle on me. Suits me just fine."

Frank grinned. "I like Tin Pan. It's a helluva lot easier on the ears."

"A name don't mean all that much anyhow. I went by Clarence Rushing for thirty years, back in Indiana. I went to college for a spell. Tried to make my living as a printer. But I kept feeling this call to see the high lonesome, these mountains, and a man just ain't happy if he ain't where he feels he belongs. I came out here looking for gold with a sluice box and a tin miner's pan. A few miners took to calling me Tin Pan on account of how much time I spent panning these streams. Hellfire, I didn't mind the new handle. I reckon it suited me. A name's just a name anyhow."

"You're right about that," Frank agreed, "unless too many folks get a hankering to see it carved on a grave marker. Then a name can mean trouble."

"Why would anybody want your name on a headstone, Frank Morgan?"

Frank looked up at the snowflakes swirling into the tiny pine grove where they were camped. "A few years back I made my living with a gun. I never killed a man who didn't need killing, but a man in that profession gets a reputation...sometimes it's one he don't deserve."

"You was a gunfighter?"

"For a time. I gave it up years ago. Tried to live peaceful, running a few cows, minding my own business on a little place down south. Some gents just won't leave a man alone when he wants it that way."

"Sounds like your past caught up to you if you're about to tangle with Ned Pine and his gang."

"They took my son. Pine, and an owlhoot named Victor Vanbergen, set out to settle old scores against me."

"Old scores?" Tin Pan asked.

"First thing they done was kill my wife, the only woman I ever loved. Then they found my boy in Durango and grabbed him for a ransom."

"Damn," Tin Pan whispered. "That's near about enough to send any man on the prowl."

"I can't just sit by and let 'em get away with it. I'm gonna finish the business they started."

"I've heard about this Vanbergen. Word is, he's got a dozen hard cases in his gang. They rob banks and trains. I didn't know they was this far north."

"They're here. I've trailed 'em a long way."

"One man won't stand much of a chance against Ned Pine and his boys. They're bad hombres. Same is bein' said about Victor Vanbergen. Have you gone plumb loco to set out after so many gunslicks?"

"Maybe," Frank sighed, sipping coffee. "My mama always told me there was something that wasn't right inside my head from the day I was born. She said I had my daddy's mean streak bred into me."

Tin Pan shrugged. "A mean streak don't sound like enough to handle so many."

"Maybe it ain't, but I damn sure intend to try. I won't let them hold my son for ransom without a fight."

Tin Pan stiffened, looking at his mule, then to the south and east. "Smother that fire, Morgan. We've got company out there someplace."

"How can you tell?" Morgan asked, cupping handfuls of snow onto the flames until the clearing was dark.

"Martha," Tin Pan replied.

"Martha?"

"Martha's my mare mule. She ain't got them big ears on top of her head for decoration. She heard something just now and it ain't no varmint. If I was you I'd fetch my rifle."

Frank jumped up and ran over to his pile of gear to jerk his Winchester free. He glanced over his shoulder at the old mountain man. "I sure hope Martha knows what she's doing," he said, hunkered down next to a pine trunk.

"She does," Tin Pan replied softly. "That ol' mule has saved my scalp from a Ute knife plenty of times."

Tin Pan pulled his ancient Sharps .52 rifle from a deerskin boot decorated with Indian beadwork. The hunting rifle's barrel was half a yard longer than Frank's Winchester, giving it long range and deadly accuracy.

"But the Utes are all south of here," Frank insisted, still watching the trees around them.

"They signed the treaty," Tin Pan agreed. "I don't figure these are Utes. Maybe you're about to get introduced to some of Ned Pine's boys."

Frank wondered if Ned Pine had sent some of his shootists back to look for Charles Bowers. If that was the case, it would give him a chance to change the long odds against him. It would make things easier.

He crept into the trees, jacking a load into the firing chamber of his Winchester saddle gun.

"Right yonder," Sam whispered. "In them pines, only it looks like the fire just went out."

"Maybe he heard us," Buster suggested.

"Could be Charlie," Tony said. "He'd be real careful if he heard a noise."

"It'd be a helluva thing if us an' Charlie started shootin' at each other in the dark," Sam said.

"How the hell are we gonna find out if it's him without gettin' our heads shot off?" Buster asked.

"I ain't got that figured yet," Sam replied. "Let's move in a little closer."

"I say we oughta spread out," Tony said.

"Good idea," Sam agreed. "Tony, you move off to the left a few dozen yards. Buster, you go to the right. Stay behind these trees until we know who it is."

"Right," Buster whispered, moving north with his rifle next to his shoulder.

Tony slipped into a thicker stand of pines

to the south of the grove where they'd spotted the flames.

Sam inched forward, blinking away snowflakes that got in his eyes. He and his partners were coming upwind, and whoever was camped ahead of them wouldn't hear a sound they made. If it was Charles Bowers who made the campfire, Sam knew he would recognize his bay stallion tied in the trees before any shots were fired.

Frank spotted a dim shape moving slowly, quietly among the trees. He didn't need a look at the man to know he was up to no good.

He thumbed back the hammer on his rifle, waiting for the man to show himself again.

The heavy roar of a big-bore rifle cracked near the mule and horses.

A shriek of pain filled the night silence. Tin Pan Rushing had hit someone with his Sharps. Frank knew the sound of the old buffalo gun. He was more than a little bit surprised that the mountain man would throw in with him in a fight that wasn't his.

Two muzzle flashes winked in the darkness from trees near the clearing. The crack of both bullets and the fingers of red flame gave Frank a target.

He squeezed off a round at a fading flash of light.

"Son of a bitch!" a deep voice cried.

Frank was ejecting a spent shell, levering another into the Winchester as fast as he could before ducking behind the tree as the voice fell silent.

"Is that you, Charlie?" someone shouted from the trees east of camp.

Now Frank was certain that some of Ned Pine's men had been sent back to look for Charles Bowers.

"Yeah, it's me!" Frank bellowed. "Is that you, Ned?"

"It's Tony. How come there's two of you shootin' at us? You shot Sam an' Buster just now."

"My cousin Clarence came up from Durango. We met on the trail. We didn't know who it was out there. Come on down to the fire. We've got coffee."

"That still don't sound like you, Charlie. Did you kill Frank Morgan?"

"Put a hole right through his chest. Sorry about shooting Sam and Buster. Come on down and we'll get the fire going again."

"Bullshit!" Tony said. "It must be you, Morgan."

"Morgan's dead, like I told you. I didn't plan on riding up to the cabin in this storm. Me and Clarence shot a wild turkey hen. Walk on down here and have some."

"You don't sound like Charlie."

"It's cold. What the hell are you so scared of, Tony?"

"Scared of bein' tricked, and I never heard you make mention of no cousin by the name of Clarence."

Tin Pan shouted from the far side of the

clearing, "I'm Charlie's cousin. I don't know who the hell you are, but you've gotta be crazy to stand out in the cold and snow. We've got coffee and roasted turkey. Come on in."

A silence followed.

"Let me check on Sam and Buster first. I can hear Buster groanin' over yonder. Ned ain't gonna like it when he finds out you shot down two of us."

"It's dark," Frank said, readying his rifle. "How the hell was I supposed to know who it was?"

"You don't sound like Charlie Bowers to me," Tony said, his voice a bit lower. "I've been ridin' with Charlie for nearly three years. I'd know his voice if I was hearin' it."

"I'll walk up there and prove it to you," Frank said. "I can't tell exactly where you are. Show yourself and I'll come up."

A dark silhouette moved in the wall of snow and pine trunks.

Frank brought his Winchester's sights up, steadying the gun against his shoulder. "I see you now, Tony. Just wait right there for me and we'll see to Sam and Buster."

He squeezed the trigger. His .44-caliber saddle gun slammed into his shoulder.

The man partly hidden by trees flipped over on his back without making a sound.

"Nice shot, Morgan," Tin Pan said from his hiding place. "Couldn't have done no better myself."

Frank stepped around the pine. "It was

163

mighty nice of him to walk out and intro-
duce himself. Some men are so damn stupid,
it makes you wonder how they stayed alive long
enough to grow out of diapers."

"One of 'em ain't dead yet," Tin Pan warned
as someone started moaning in the night.

"I'm always real careful," Frank replied as
he headed into the forest.

Twenty

Tin Pan lit a small railroad conductor's lantern
before he followed Frank into the trees. Yellow
light and tree trunk shadows wavered across
the snow as they walked with their backs to
the wind and snow.

"The one that's moanin' is over here," Tin
Pan said, raising his lantern higher to cast more
light on the few inches of snow covering the
ground.

"I hear him," Frank said, covering their
progress with his Peacemaker.

"Hope he ain't in good enough shape to use
his gun," Tin Pan said.

"He won't be," Frank assured him.

The first body they came to was a stumpy
cowboy wearing a sheepskin coat. He lay in
a patch of bloody snow. His chest was not
moving.

"This is the feller I shot," Tin Pan said.

"I got the one who called himself Tony. He's

farther to the right. Let's see what the live one has to say," Frank said with a look to the east. "The other two won't have much when it comes to words. I can hear the last one making some noise. Let's find him first."

"That'll be Sam or Buster," Tin Pan remembered.

"I don't give a damn what his name is. I'm gonna make him talk to me, if he's able," Frank replied, aiming for the groaning sounds.

A dark lump lay in the snow. Frank could hear horses in the trees about a hundred yards away, stamping a hoof now and then, made nervous by the gunshots.

He came to the body of a man lying on his back, his mouth open, a rifle held loosely in his right hand. Blood oozed from his lips onto the flattened hat brim behind his head. The man groaned again.

Frank knelt beside him as Tin Pan held the lantern above his head.

"Howdy, friend," Frank said.

Buster's pain-glazed eyes moved to Frank's face.

"You ain't Charlie," he stammered.

"Nope. I sure as hell ain't Charlie. Mr. Bowers and I met back on the trail. I shot him. Put him on his horse headed for Durango. That's fifty hard miles in a storm like this. A man would bet long odds against him making it all that way, in the shape he's in. He's probably dead by now. But I gave him the chance to save his ass...if he's tough enough to make that ride to Durango."

"You're...Frank Morgan."

"I am."

"We thought it was Charlie's fire we seen."

"You were mistaken. You and your pardners made another big mistake when you tried to jump me. Tony, and some other fella who was with you, are both dead."

"That'll be Tony and Sam. I told both of 'em we oughta be careful sneaking up on your fire."

The light from Tin Pan's lantern showed the pain on Buster's face. A bullet hole in his chest leaked blood, and by the amount of blood coming from Buster's mouth, Frank knew the bullet had pierced a lung.

"I need to know about Ned Pine's hideout, and my son, Conrad Browning. Is my boy okay?" Frank asked, his deep voice with an edge to it.

"Ned's gonna kill him...but only after he lures you up there so he can kill you." Buster issued his warning between gasps for air.

"I'm a hard man to kill, Buster. How many men has Pine got with him?"

"Maybe thirteen more. You ain't got a chance, Morgan. If Ned don't get you himself, then Lyle or Slade will. They're guarding your boy. Lyle is as good with a gun as any man on earth. Slade's just as good." Buster paused and winced. "Jesus, my chest hurts. I can't hardly breathe." He coughed up blood, shivering, unable to move his limbs.

"How many men are guarding the entrance into the canyon?" Frank asked.

"To hell with you, Morgan. Find out for yourself. See if you don't get killed."

Frank brought the barrel of the Peacemaker down to Buster's mouth and held the muzzle against his gritted teeth. "I'm only gonna ask you one more time, Buster, and then I'm gonna blow the top of your head off. How many men are guarding the entrance to the canyon?"

Buster stared at the pistol in Frank's hand. "I'm gonna die anyway, 'less you take me to a doctor."

"Ain't many doctors in these mountains. A few hours ago your pardner, Charlie Bowers, was wanting one real bad. About all I can do for you is put you on your horse and send you toward Durango tonight, like I did Charles Bowers. You feel like you can make a fifty-mile ride?"

"I'll freeze to death, if I don't bleed to death first. I need some whiskey."

"I've got whiskey in my saddlebags. Good Kentucky sour mash too. Now I'm not saying I'd waste any of it on you, but your chances are better if you tell me what I want to know about who's guarding the entrance to that canyon."

"Josh. Josh and Arnie are watchin' the canyon from a rock pile at the top."

"Has Ned or any of the others injured my boy?" Frank tapped Buster's front teeth with his pistol barrel to add a bit of emphasis to his question.

"Ned slapped him around some..." Buster broke into another fit of bloody coughing.

167

"Ned's after you. He swore he was gonna kill you. He won't kill your boy until he sees you lyin' dead someplace."

"Damn," Tin Pan sighed, balancing his Sharps in the palm of his hand. "That Pine's a rotten bastard, to hold a kid as bait like he is."

"Gimme...some of that whiskey, like you promised," Buster said.

"I didn't promise you anything, Buster," Frank said, taking his gun away from Buster's teeth. "I only said I had some in my saddlebags. If I poured a swallow down your throat, it'd just leak out onto the snow on account of that big hole in your chest. I think I'll save my whiskey for a better occasion. Be a shame to waste good sour mash on a man who's gonna be dead in a few minutes."

"You bastard," Buster hissed.

"I've been called worse," Frank replied. "But I've never been one to be wasteful. I grew up mighty poor. Pouring whiskey into a dying man is damn sure a waste of the distiller's fine art."

"Are you just gonna leave me here to die?" Buster croaked, blood bubbling from his lips.

"There's another way," Frank said.

Buster blinked. "What the hell are you talkin' about, Morgan?"

"I can put a bullet through your brain and you won't be cold or hurt anymore."

"That'd be murder."

"Ned and the rest of you killed my wife. That was murder. In case you don't read the Bible, it says to take an eye for an eye."

"You ain't got no conscience, Morgan. Ned told us you was a rotten son of a bitch."

"I've got no conscience when it comes to men who kill women and harm kids who can't defend themselves. To tell the truth, killing you and Pine and all of his gang will be a downright pleasure."

"Jesus...you ain't really gonna do it, are you?" Buster whispered.

Frank stood up, holstering his Colt. "I damn sure am unless they give me back my son."

"Put me on my horse, Morgan. Give me a fightin' chance to live."

"It don't appear you can sit a horse, Buster, but if you want I can tie you across your saddle."

Tin Pan shook his head. "Hell, Morgan, this sumbitch is already dead. Leave him where he lays. Have you forgot that him an' his partners just tried to kill you?"

"I'm a forgiving man," Frank said dryly. "Just because some gunslick tries to take away all you have, or all you're ever gonna have, don't mean you can't show any forgiveness for what he tried to do." He gazed down at Buster for a time. "Are you truly sorry you tried to kill me?" he asked.

"Hell, no," Buster spat, still defiant. "If I'd had the right shot at you, it'd be you layin' in this snow with a hole in your guts."

Frank chuckled, but there was no humor in it. He glanced over at Tin Pan. "See what I mean?" he asked. "We've got a killer here with no remorse. I think I'll just leave him here to die slow. His pardners are already dead. We'll take their horses and deliver 'em to Ned Pine. Send them into that canyon with empty saddles, a little message from me that this fight has just started."

"It's your fight," Tin Pan said.

Frank slapped the old mountain man on the shoulder. "I'm glad I had you siding with me. You dropped that outlaw quicker'n snuff makes spit."

"It was the coffee," Tin Pan replied. "A man who'll offer a stranger a cup of coffee with brown sugar in it way up in these slopes deserves a helping hand."

Frank gave Tin Pan a genuine laugh. "Let's fetch their horses down to our picket line. Feel free to take any of their guns you want. Where they're going, they won't be needing a pistol or a rifle."

Tin Pan grinned. "Reckon we could add a splash of that Kentucky sour mash to the next cup of coffee?"

"You can have all of it you want."

Buster coughed again, then his feet began to twitch in death throes.

"You see what I was talking about?" Frank asked. "It would have been a waste of good bottled spirits to pour even one drop of it into a dead man."

"What makes a printer from Indiana get filled with wanderlust for the mountains?" Frank asked, drinking coffee laced with whiskey after the outlaws' horses had been tied in the trees along with Frank's animals, and the mule.

"Dreamin', I reckon. I saw tintypes of the Rockies and I just knew I had to see 'em for myself."

"And you planned to pay for it by panning for gold in these high mountain streams?"

"There was a gold rush on back then. Men were finding gold nuggets as big as marbles."

"But you never found any," Frank said.

"Not even a flake of placer gold. This country had been panned out by the time I got here. The only other way is to dig into these rocky slopes. I never was much for using a pick and a shovel."

"So you've turned to trapping?"

"It's a living. I'm happy up here, just me and old Martha for company. I had me a Ute squaw once, only she ran off with a miner who had gold in his purse."

"I owe Martha a sack of corn," Frank remembered. "She heard this bad bunch sneaking up on us."

Tin Pan smiled. "Martha earns her keep. She can tote three hundred pounds of cured pelts and she don't ever complain. Once in a while she gets ornery and won't cross a creek if it's up to its banks, but I reckon that just shows good sense."

"You don't get lonely up here?"

"Naw. There's a few of us old mountain men still prowling these peaks. We get together once in a while to swap tales and catch up."

"I think I understand," Frank told him. "I've got a dog. I call him Dog. He's better company than most humans. I've had him for quite a spell."

"Same goes for Martha," Tin Pan said, glancing into the pines where his mule and the horses were tied. "She's right decent company, when she ain't in the mood to kick me if I don't get the packsaddle on just right."

Frank chuckled. "I want you to know I'm grateful for you helping me with those gunmen."

Tin Pan gave him a steady gaze. "You're takin' on too much, Morgan, tryin' to go after thirteen more of 'em all by your lonesome."

"I don't have much of a choice. They're holding my son hostage. I can't turn my back on it."

"Maybe you do have a choice," Tin Pan said after he gave it some thought.

"How's that?"

"I might just throw in with you to help get that boy of yours away from Ned Pine. I ain't no gunfighter, but I can damn sure shoot a rifle. If I find a spot on the rim of that canyon, I can take a few of 'em down with my Sharps."

"It isn't your fight," Frank said. "But I'm grateful for the offer anyhow."

"I've been in fights that wasn't mine before," Tin Pan declared. "Let me study on it some. I'll let you know in the morning what I've decided to do. I'd have to ask Martha about it. She don't like loud noises, like guns."

Twenty-one

Josh Winslow and Arnie Sims sat inside a circle of boulders above the mouth of Lone Pine Canyon.

Winslow was wanted in New Mexico Territory for bank robbery and murder. Sims had warrants out for him in Arkansas and Texas for murder.

"It's cold up here," Josh said.

"Damn right it is," Arnie agreed. "Ned said we couldn't have no fire on account of Morgan. He might see the flames or smell the smoke."

"Morgan's probably dead by now."

"Then where the hell is Charlie?" Arnie asked, rubbing his hands together. "And how come we ain't seen hide nor hair of Sam and Buster and Tony?"

"Charlie most likely made camp to wait out this storm. Same goes for the others. A horse don't travel too good into a wind full of snow."

"Charlie didn't have no provisions with him, just some whiskey and jerky. He'd ride hard for the cabin if he could. I'm sure of it."

"You're sayin' Frank Morgan got Charles Bowers? Nobody ever put so much as a nick in Charlie's hide. He's the most careful man I ever knew."

"All the same, he shoulda been here by now. It's damn near dawn. The others shoulda been back. I've got a bad feelin' about this."

Josh took a pint bottle of whiskey out of his coat. "Have some more red-eye. It'll make the waitin' easier. Roger and Jerry are supposed to come up here to relieve us after it gets light."

Arnie took the bottle and drank a thirsty gulp. Then he took a deep breath. "This here's the best invention since the gun, Josh. A man can't hardly live without it. I sure as hell hope them boys down at the cabin didn't drink the rest all up before we get there."

"Whiskey helps," Josh agreed, peering over the top of a boulder at the snow-laden mouth of the canyon below. "Hell, ain't nobody in his right mind gonna ride through this wind and snowfall tonight."

"How come Ned's so dead set on killin' Morgan?"

"It goes way back. Ned and Victor killed Morgan's woman and he came after 'em. Morgan killed a bunch of men in Vanbergen's gang and some of the boys who rode with Ned. Ned and Victor ain't never got over it. They want revenge for what Morgan did to 'em."

"Sounds like Morgan's the one with a reason for revenge, if you ask me. That was before I throwed in with Ned. I was just comin' out of Fort Smith at the time."

"I was there," Josh remembered. "Morgan's a killer, a damn good shootist."

"I used to hear stories about him. That was years ago, before I took up the outlaw trail. Folks said he was meaner'n a longhorn bull on the prod, and that nobody was any faster with a six-gun."

"He's just a man," Josh said, taking his own swallow of whiskey. "You can kill damn near any sumbitch if you go about it right."

"I hope Charlie got him," Arnie said.

"Maybe they killed each other."

"That could be what's taking Sam and the others so long, lookin' for the bodies in all this snow."

Josh leaned back against the rock with a blanket thrown over him. "That kid of Morgan's ain't got any backbone. When Ned started knockin' him around, he cried like a damn sugar-tit baby."

"I'll agree he ain't much," Arnie said. "Makes a man wonder why Morgan would go to all this trouble."

"I figure Morgan's dead by now. Soon as Ned is satisfied, we can kill the kid and head back south where it's warmer to rob a few banks an' trains. This here cold weather don't agree with me."

"It hurts my joints," Arnie complained. "I hate this cold. Soon as this business with Morgan is over, Ned promised we'd ride down to Texas."

"I've been asking him to head for the Mexican border so we can get ourselves some pretty *señoritas*."

"That damn sure sounds good on a night like this, sittin' up here at the top of this canyon without no fire. We're liable to freeze to death."

"It's gonna be light soon," Josh said. "That fire in the potbelly down at the cabin is sure gonna feel good." He closed his eyes, pulling his hat brim over his face. "You keep an eye on that canyon mouth for a spell. I'm gonna try an' get me some shut-eye."

"It's too damn cold to sleep," Arnie said. "Pass me back that whiskey so I can stay warm."

"I'm gonna throw in with you," Tin Pan said. "Made up my mind on it."

"No need, unless you're just restless, or itching for a fight."

"Got nothing to do with restlessness, Morgan. I've been thinking about that eighteen-year-old boy of yours, and the way things are stacked against you."

"I've never been one to worry about the odds," Frank said as he placed more sticks underneath the coffeepot. The smell of coffee filled the clearing.

"There's times when it pays to worry a little."

"Maybe," Frank replied.

Skies brightened to the east. The snow had stopped falling and the wind had died down.

"I'll show you that old Ute trail down the back side of the canyon," Tin Pan continued. "If I stay perched up in them rocks with my Sharps, I can get a few of 'em."

"I'm obliged for the offer, but there's no need to put your neck in a noose over me. I can handle whatever's up there on my own."

"You're a hardheaded cuss."

Coffee was boiling out of the spout, and Frank put on a glove to take it off the flames, placing it on a rock beside the crackling fire.

"I've been told that before," he said, grinning. "It comes from my daddy's side of the family."

Tin Pan drew a Bowie knife from a sheath inside his right boot. "I'll slice up some of that fatback and put chunks of turkey with it. Oughta make a decent meal."

"Sounds mighty good to me." Frank added a handful of snow to the coffeepot to get the grounds to settle to the bottom. "We can get moving soon as there's light enough to see. That's a Bowie you're carrying. I've got one of my own. Best knife on earth for killing a man."

"Mine's skinned many a grizzly and elk. I know the way to the canyon real well," Tin Pan said, pulling a chunk of salted pork from a waxed paper bundle, then cutting thin slices off with his knife. "Trapped it a few times."

"Is there any cover on the floor of that canyon?" Frank asked.

"Scrub pines. Not many. If Ned decides to hole up in the cabin and wait you out, it'll take an army to flush him out of there."

"I've got plenty of ammunition," Frank declared, "some with forty grains of powder in 'em. When I start filling that cabin with lead, they'll come out after a spell."

"Sounds like you've done this sort of thing before, Morgan."

"A few times."

Tin Pan frowned. "Do it ever bother you, thinkin' about the men you've killed?"

Frank wagged his head. "Like I told you before, I never killed a man who didn't deserve it."

Tin Pan laid strips of fatback in Frank's small frying pan and added a few pieces of turkey. He set it on a flat stone close to the flames, nestling it into the glowing coals. "That oughta do it," he said, wiping his knife clean on one leg of his stained deerskin pants.

"Coffee's ready," Frank said, glancing up at a gray sky paling with dawn.

He poured himself a cup, then another for the mountain man, tossing him the cotton bag of brown sugar.

"Fit for a king," Tin Pan said with a smile. "It don't get much better than this."

"You're right," Frank agreed. "Open country, a warm fire, and good vittles."

"Don't forget about the coffee."

Frank slurped a steaming mouthful from his cup. "I hadn't forgotten about it."

The salt pork began to sizzle in the skillet, giving off a wonderful smell. But Frank's thoughts were on Conrad, what he was most likely going through now. Ned Pine would torture him, making him as miserable as possible, asking questions about Frank the boy couldn't answer. He and Frank barely knew each other, and the circumstances under which Conrad was born, without Frank being there, made the boy resentful. Conrad didn't know the whole story behind his birth and his father's love for his mother.

A back way into the box canyon would give Frank a tremendous advantage, and with a shooter up on the rim, things could get hot for Pine and his bunch. Frank owed the old mountain man for his willingness to lend a hand.

The first order of business would be to take out the two riflemen guarding the entrance. If he made his approach very carefully, he could take them without making much noise. Then he'd make his way down the Ute trail behind the cabin and start the serious business of saving Conrad, killing off Pine's men one or two at a time.

Tin Pan turned over the fatback strips with the point of his knife.

"Won't be long now," the old man said.

"My belly's rubbing against my backbone now," Frank replied, taking another sip of coffee.

Roger Clements and Jerry Page were still drunk from a night-long consumption of whiskey.

Page was from Tennessee, wanted for a string of robberies in his home state. Clements had been a paid assassin for the Knights of the Golden Circle in Mississippi, killing seven men after the war without anyone knowing his identity.

Jerry looked up at darkening skies. "I thought this storm was gonna blow over.

Looks like more of this goddamn snow is headed our way."

"Just our luck," Roger muttered. "We'll freeze our asses off up here if that wind builds."

Jerry glimpsed a shadow moving among the boulders behind them. "Who the hell is that?"

Roger turned the direction Jerry was pointing. "I don't see nothin'. You're imagining things."

"I was sure I saw somebody headed toward us."

"Who the hell would it be?"

"This bad light plays tricks on a man's eyes. I wish the hell the sun would come out."

"Make a wish in one hand an' take a crap in the other. See which one fills up first."

"Pass me that whiskey," Jerry said. "Could be I'm just too cold."

Roger handed Jerry the bottle. Half of its contents were missing.

Jerry had raised the bottle to his lips, when suddenly a dark shape appeared on top of the boulder behind Roger.

An object came twirling through the air toward Jerry, and then something struck his chest. "Son of a..." he cried, driven back in the snow by a Bowie knife buried in his gut just below his breastbone.

"What the hell?" Roger cried, scrambling to his feet as Jerry slumped to the ground.

A heavy rifle barrel slammed into the back of Roger's head and he sank to his knees, losing consciousness before he fell over on his face.

Jerry cried, "What happened?"

The shape of a man stood over him.

"Who...the hell...are you?"

"Frank Morgan," a deep voice said.

"Oh, no. We was supposed...to be watchin' for you."

"You weren't watching close enough, and now you'll pay for it with your life."

"Please don't...kill me. I've got a wife back home."

"You're already dead, cowboy. The tip of my knife is buried in your heart."

Waves of pain filled Jerry's chest. "No!" he whimpered, feeling warm blood flow down the front of his shirt.

"I'm gonna cut your pardner's throat," the voice said. "He has to die, for what you've done to my son."

"It was...Ned's idea," Jerry croaked.

"You went along with it," the tall man said, bending down to jerk his knife from Jerry's chest.

As Jerry's eyes were closing, he saw Frank Morgan walk over to Roger. With a single slashing motion, Morgan whipped the knife across Roger's throat.

Jerry's eyes batted shut. He didn't feel the cold now.

Twenty-two

Tiny snowflakes fell in sheets across the log cabin. The bottom of the canyon floor was covered with several inches of white.

An eerie silence gripped the box canyon as Frank made his way down slippery rocks and sheer cliffs, following the old Ute trail Tin Pan had showed him.

Smoke curled from a rock chimney as Frank watched the shack, after he'd made slow but careful progress across the valley. Behind the cabin, more than a dozen horses stood with their tails to the wind in crude pole corrals. A pile of hay stood in one corner.

He moved quietly through the scrub pines. To the north Tin Pan was covering the hideout from a cluster of rocks at a range of more than five hundred yards.

"I hope he's a good shot from a distance," Frank said under his breath, slipping among the trees. The gray-bearded mountain man had proved to be an excellent marksman, but from the top of the canyon he'd have to be better than most men to hit anything, even with a long-range rifle like his Sharps .52 buffalo gun.

Frank thought about Conrad. Would Ned Pine kill the boy when he heard the first gunshot? Frank had never really known the boy, due to circumstances beyond his control and the distance between them.

He wondered if attacking the cabin would put Conrad's life in danger.

"It's a chance I've got to take," Frank said, creeping closer to the cabin.

The patter of small snowflakes rattled on his hat brim, and the crunch of new-fallen snow came from his boots when he put his feet down.

"No way to do this quiet," Frank said, still being careful with the placement of each foot.

A horse snorted in the corrals. Frank remained motionless behind a pine trunk until the animal settled. A range-bred horse would notice him making an advance toward the cabin. A horse raised in a stable wouldn't pay him any mind. There was a big difference in horses... Frank had always preferred the range-bred variety.

A blast of northerly wind swept across the top of the canyon, and Frank knew that old Tin Pan Rushing was freezing his ass off, waiting for things to start.

A bit of luck, Frank thought, to run across the mountain man when he least expected to find any help getting his son away from Ned Pine. While he usually worked alone when he was employing his guns, it was a comfort to know Clarence Rushing was up there with his rifle.

Moving carefully toward the back of the cabin, he sighted an outhouse behind the place, nestled against the trunk of a small ponderosa pine.

The snowfall grew heavier.

"Maybe I can catch one or two taking a piss," Frank said under his breath.

He moved closer to the outhouse. Thing were

too quiet and that had an unsettling effect on him. But the silence could also be a blessing if he used it to his advantage.

Scott Warren had been drinking all night and most of the morning. He felt like his bladder was about to burst open any minute. He was wanted for bank robbery down in Texas, and for a killing in Indian Territory involving a trading post operator and his wife.

Scott stood over the two-holer, letting his steamy water flow into the hole dug beneath the wood seats. This waiting for Ned Pine's adversary was getting the best of him, and there was no money to be made from killing an old gunfighter like Frank Morgan. Unless there was a profit in it, Scott had little patience for personal grudges. Ned was out of his head with a need for vengeance against this shootist named Morgan, a gunman well past his prime. None of this made any sense to a man like Scott.

"That's better," he sighed, when his bladder finally emptied into the pit.

Pale light suddenly flooded the outhouse. Scott turned to see who had opened the door.

A knife blade slipped between his ribs, he only caught a glimpse of the figure who stood behind him.

Without buttoning the front of his pants, Scott jerked his Walker Colt .44 free and staggered outside, cocking the hammer with blood cascading down the back of his mackinaw in regular spurts.

"You sneaky son of a bitch!" Scott cried, unable to find the man who had knifed him.

With nothing to aim at, Scott let the Walker drop to his side as chains of white-hot agony shot through his liver. As a reflex, his muscles tightened before he started to fall to the ground.

His trigger finger curled. A deafening explosion filled the box canyon, followed by a howl of pain when Scott Warren, a professional gunman by trade, shot himself in the right foot with his own .44-caliber slug.

"Damn, damn, damn!" Scott shrieked, hopping around on his good leg, spraying blood all over the snow from both of his wounds.

"What the hell was that?" a voice demanded from a back door of the log cabin.

Scott was in too much pain to answer.

"Lookee yonder," another whiskey-thick voice said. "Scott went an' shot hisself in the leg."

"Wonder why he did that. All he said he was gonna do was take a piss..."

"He's dead drunk, Josh. When a man's that drunk he's liable to do anything."

Scott continued to hop around in a circle, reaching for his bloody boot.

"What'll we do, Mack?"

"Let the dumb sumbitch dance out there in the snow. If he ain't got enough sense to keep from shootin' himself, then let him jump up and down."

As Mack spoke, a rifle thundered from a stand

of pines behind the cabin. Mack Brown, a horse thief from Arizona Territory, fell down in a heap in the cabin doorway with his hands gripping his belly.

Josh Winslow was trying to get out of the way when the next gunshot rang out. Something hot hit him in the back, pushing him forward into the door frame of the shack with the force of impact.

"I'm hit!" Josh screamed as he sank to his knees with blood squirting from his shirtfront.

Men inside the cabin began scrambling for their guns.

Frank moved away into the curtain of snow. The sound of his rifle still echoed among the scrub ponderosa pines where he'd fired at Josh.

Frank found a new hiding place fifty yards to the north. Five more of Ned Pine's men were out of the fight, and the war had just begun.

He moved silently, deeper in the forest behind the cabin, to make his next play.

A thundering gunshot roared from the rim of the canyon and a man in front of the cabin let out a scream. Curtis Johnson, a hired killer and stagecoach bandit from Waco, ended his cry with a wail as he fell down in the snow with his hand clamped around the walnut grips of his pistol.

"Tin Pan's good," Frank told himself in a

feathery whisper when he saw the man go down at the front cabin door. "I'm not sure I could have made that shot myself. Helluva lot of range for any long gun."

A barrel-chested cowboy came out the back door with a rifle, a Winchester Yellow Boy, clutched to his shoulder. He swept his gunsights back and forth.

Frank took careful aim and pulled the trigger on his Winchester.

The cowboy did a curious spin before firing a harmless shot into the treetops.

Arnie Sims went down slowly, his eyes bulging from their sockets, wishing he'd stayed in New Orleans instead of joining Ned Pine's outlaw gang last year.

"Shit," Arnie gulped, falling over on his face in the snow with his rifle underneath him. Winking lights clouded his vision until his eyelids closed.

Frank jacked another shell into his saddle gun.

"Everybody stay put!" a muffled voice commanded from inside the cabin. "Don't show yourselves. It's gotta be Morgan. I'm gonna kill his boy if one more shot gets fired!"

Ned Pine's gray eyebrows knitted. He peered through a window of the cabin.

"How the hell did Morgan get past Bowers?" Lyle asked in a grating voice.

"How the hell should I know," Pine spat, finding nothing among the scrub pines encircling the shack. "Charlie is good at what he does...maybe the best."

"He ain't all that good," Slade answered, watching the back door where Arnie lay trembling in the snow. "Ask ol' Arnie here if Bowers was good at bushwhackin'."

"Shut up!" Pine snapped. "There's another shooter up on the rim."

"I thought you said Morgan always worked alone," Lyle remembered.

"He does. That's what I can't figure," Pine replied, his pale eyes moving across the Pine Canyon rim.

Slade's eyelids slitted. "Ain't heard no fire from Jerry or Roger."

"Morgan probably got to both of 'em," Lyle suggested, "or the other bastard shootin' at us got 'em. We don't know who the hell he could be."

"Wonder what happened to Sam, Buster, an' Tony," Don Jones said, facing a window. "They shoulda been back by now if they had any luck."

"Luck's a funny thing," Lyle said. "Lady Luck smiles on some folks and purely shits on some others. Sam an' his boys may have run into Lady Luck when she was in a bad mood. They all oughta been back here by now."

Slade leaned against the door frame. "My daddy always said that if a man is lucky, cow shit will do for brains. Charlie an' Sam and his boys are all dead."

"What the hell would you know about it?" Pine cried, both hands filled with iron.

Slade was not disturbed by Ned's question, nor was he disturbed by Pine's bad reputation. "I'm an authority on luck, good and bad, Ned. I say our luck just ran out. Whoever this bastard Morgan is, he's good. It'll take a lot of luck for us to kill him."

Ned backed away from the window. "Untie that kid and bring him to me. We'll see if Morgan is willing to shoot through his own flesh and blood to settle a score."

Don Jones leaned against the windowpane. "There ain't nobody out there," he said.

Seconds later a bullet smashed the glass in front of his face. A slug from a .52-caliber buffalo gun entered his right eye.

"Damn!" Rich Boggs said when Don was flung away from the window.

Don Jones went to the dirt floor of the cabin with the back of his skull hanging by tendons and tissue. A plug of his brains lay beside the potbelly stove. A twist of his long black hair clung to the skull fragment.

"Holy shit!" Rich cried backing away to the center of the room. "Them's Don's brains hangin' out."

"Shut up!" Ned bellowed. "Untie that kid and bring him to me."

"Why's that?" Lyle wondered aloud.

"We're gonna see if Mr. Morgan is all that quick to take a shot at his son when I'm using him for a human shield. Bring him to me!"

"Right, Boss," Rich answered, moving carefully over to a straight-backed chair where Conrad Browning was bound hand and foot.

"Douse them lanterns," Pine instructed. "I'll walk this kid outside with my pistol under his throat while the rest of you saddle our horses."

"We're pulling out?" Slade asked.

Ned nodded. "For now. We'll find a better place to fight Morgan, after we join up with Victor and his boys."

"What makes you think Morgan will let us ride out?" Lyle asked.

"It's real simple," Ned explained. "Morgan followed us all this way to save his snot-nosed kid. He won't take the chance that I'll kill his son. Bring that kid over here. I'll walk out in plain sight with my gun under his jaw."

Twenty-three

Victor Vanbergen sat at a table inside the Wagon Wheel Saloon in Cortez, Colorado Territory. He and his men had ridden to town from their hideout at Gypsum Gap to buy staples, and more whiskey for the cold nights ahead.

It was darkening outside, and snow was falling. It had been a rough trip for Vic's men across the eastern edge of the badlands.

"Let's stay the night in town," said Ford Peters, a former Confederate cavalryman who served time with Bloody Bill Anderson's raiders during the war. "It'll be a helluva cold ride back to Gypsum Gap in this snow. Hell, this is March and I can't figure why

190

it's still snowing this time of year. A man could get to where he don't like this cold country. To tell the truth, Vic, I ain't taken much of a shine to it."

"Relax," Vic said. "This town's got a sheriff and a telegraph line. If Morgan trailed us instead of Ned, there'll be a killin' to explain. Ned told us wait for him at the old mining town, an' that's damn sure what we're gonna do. Ned's real smart when it comes to these things. He's been in more tight spots than all of us put together, and he knows what to do when things get tough."

"It's just so damn cold," Ford replied.

Vernon Jenkins, a killer from Alabama, nodded. "It's too damn cold to be ridin' a horse, Vic. Ned an' his bunch will take care of Morgan, if Charlie Bowers didn't get him on our back trail, an' that'll be the end of it. I say we stay here where it's warm. Where there's plenty of women an' whiskey an' decent food. I'm tired of the crap Larry fixes us. I've never seen so damn many beans in my life. Larry can't cook worth a shit, if you ask me."

Vic was about to put both men in their places when the front doors to the Wagon Wheel opened. A man in a duster coat, a derby hat, and lace-up shoes came in with snow dusting his shoulders and his hat brim.

"Could that stranger be the law, like a federal marshal or a goddamn Pinkerton detective or somethin'?" Ford asked softly, letting his right hand drop below the tabletop near the butt of his pistol.

"He ain't armed," Vic said, watching the new-comer pull off his coat. "You're too damn edgy tonight, Ford. Have another drink of whiskey. I've never seen you so goddamn jumpy before, for no reason."

But when the stranger in the derby spotted Vic and Ford and Vern seated at the table, he made straight for them with his duster over his arm. He sported a Van Dyke beard with a touch of gray in his sideburns.

"Excuse me, gentlemen," he said. "My name is Louis Pettigrew. I'm a reporter, a writer from Boston. I wondered if you might be able to tell me where I can find a gunfighter, a man by the name of Frank Morgan."

"Maybe we've never heard of him," Vic answered. "What the hell is a reporter from up in Boston doin' looking for old Frank Morgan?"

"He's a famous man. A shootist, or a pistolman as they call them in Missouri. I wanted an interview with him...to find out if all the stories about him are true. I was told he was in this area now."

"I think he's dead," Vic said.

Pettigrew shook his head. "I just spoke with a city marshal over in Durango, a man by the name of Dickson. He said that Frank Morgan is very much alive, and that he's off on some quest to save his estranged son, a young man he's only seen once or twice since the boy was born. I took notes. The boy's mother was killed a long time ago."

Vic gave Ford and Vern a sideways look. "I

don't think that marshal knows what he's talkin' about. We heard it on good authority that Morgan was killed south of here. Somebody shot him an' nobody knows who done it."

"Oh, my lord," Pettigrew sighed, dusting snowflakes from the brim of his bowler. "I suppose I've arrived too late. I really wanted to hear Mr. Morgan's story. He's known as one of the last gunfighters in the West."

"I think his reputation was bigger'n he was," Vic said evenly.

"Not according to my sources," Pettigrew went on. "I've checked the records. Morgan has killed more than forty men, and that puts him in the same category as that boy madman from Texas, John Wesley Hardin. Hardin is in prison now, studying law, and he won't grant any interviews. Frank Morgan is said to be the last of the old-time gunslingers. I wanted to write his life story."

"Morgan wasn't much," Ford said. "I knew him."

"He wasn't much?" Pettigrew asked. "What do you mean by that remark?"

"He was nothin' but a back-shooter, a bushwhacker. I never met anybody who saw him go face-to-face with a real gunman who knew his business."

"Interesting," Pettigrew said. "Can you tell me more about him?"

"He was a lowlife. A hired assassin. He never cared how he killed a man. He wasn't honorable. He'd just as soon shoot a man in the back as sneeze."

Pettigrew scowled. "That doesn't fit with what others have told me about him."

"Like I told you," Ford replied "I knew the sorry son of a bitch. He was no good, and he deserved to be planted in the ground. One thing's for sure, he damn sure wasn't no gunfighter."

"Would you be willing to give me some details regarding his life?" Pettigrew asked. "I'll gladly pay you for your time. My paper, the *Boston Globe*, will reimburse me. If Morgan is dead, as you say, then you may be the only source I have to set the record straight."

Ford gave Vic a sideways look. "I'll tell you plenty about him, Mr. Pettigrew. Only, you're wrong about him bein' a famous gunslinger. He was just an ordinary man with no courage. He shot most of his victims in the back. How much will you pay me to tell you about him?"

"But I've heard so many stories... I think my newspaper will go as high as twenty-five dollars for the facts surrounding Morgan's reputation."

"Mostly bullshit," Ford said, as Vern gave him a wink and a half smile. "His reputation as a gunslinger was mostly bullshit, a bunch of half-truths. Every time some son of a bitch tells a story, it gets bigger."

"May I join you at your table?" Pettigrew asked. "I'll pay for a round of drinks."

"Take a seat," Ford said. "I'm about to tell you the truth about Frank Morgan, only I don't think you're gonna like what I have to say, since you think he was so all-fired famous as a gunman. But first off, let me see the color of your money. Put the twenty-five dollars down on the table or I won't say another word."

Pettigrew pulled back a chair, reaching into his pants pocket. He took twenty-five silver dollars and placed them on the table in front of Ford. "All I want is the truth," he said, settling down in his wooden chair.

"You're about to hear the truth about Frank Morgan," Ford said, enjoying himself. "It's mostly a pack of lies, what folks say about him. He was yellow all the way through. He never braced a man in a contest at the draw. I know that for an honest fact."

"My editor will be disappointed," Pettigrew said, taking a pad and pencil from his coat. "However, my story must be accurate, down to the last detail. First of all, please give me your name as my source."

"I'm Ford Peters."

"And what is your profession, Mr. Peters?"

Vern chuckled and turned to a window to hide the mirth on his face.

"I'm a cattleman by trade," Ford said. "How about that round of drinks?"

Pettigrew finished his notations, then turned toward the bar and waved his hand in the air. "Drinks all around!" he shouted.

Vic knew Ford would fill the newsman's ears with falsehoods and outright lies. He laughed inwardly. It was a way to spend a snowy evening in the badlands of Colorado Territory, filling the reporter's head with fanciful notions.

There would be no one to refute Ford's accounts of Frank Morgan's exploits. Vic was certain that Morgan was dead by now, with Charles Bowers lying in ambush for him on the trail up from Durango. Morgan was an old man, well past his prime, and Charlie was as good as they come at putting men in their graves. He had never made a mistake...not Charles. Frank Morgan was a dead man by now.

"He made a name for himself down in Texas," Ford began, "but he's ridden all over the western territories. He wears a brace of pistols. His favorite weapon is a Colt Peacemaker forty-five and a forty-four-forty saddle gun. Like I told you before, he's a back-shooter, so a rifle is what he uses most. He can shoot a man from three hundred yards away without ever havin' to show himself."

"I've heard dozens of stories about his quick draw," Pettigrew said.

"A pack of lies," Ford replied. "He's slow on the draw an' he won't face a good gunman in a showdown. I'd say he's a man who knows his limitations."

"How well did you know him?"

"We were close. Nearly like brothers right after the war. He was a small-time thief. Frank was yellow, when it came down to cases. He'd rob an unarmed man or steal cattle an' horses from some poor farmer when he was dead sure he had the advantage."

"That doesn't sound like the same man I've been told about," Pettigrew said, taking notes as fast as he could write. "In some parts of the country, Frank Morgan's gunmanship is almost legendary."

"It's bullshit," Ford said.

"How can so many other people be wrong?" Pettigrew asked, his brow furrowing.

Ford laughed. "They didn't know him the way I did," he said matter-of-factly.

"How did you come to know Morgan so well?" Pettigrew asked, his pencil poised above his pad.

Vic wondered how Ford would answer this question, since Ford only knew Morgan by reputation.

A balding barkeep brought over three glasses of whiskey on a tray.

"And what's for you, sir?" the bartender asked Pettigrew.

"Brandy."

"We ain't got no brandy. Red wine is all we've got, unless you want this here whiskey."

"I'll have the whiskey," Pettigrew said.

The barman put their drinks down. Vic tried to hide a smile, for the arrival of their drinks would give Ford Peters enough time to come up with some sort of answer to the newpaperman's question, how it was that he knew Frank Morgan when he didn't know him at all.

"Like I was about to say," Ford continued, "I knew Frank down in Texas." He tossed back his drink. "Morgan was a hired gun, only he wasn't much good at it."

"He wasn't as good as his reputation?" Pettigrew asked with a startled look on his face.

"He went up against Shorty Russel down in Brownwood. Shorty wasn't any great shakes as a gunman. Shorty drew first an' put a lead slug through Morgan's shoulder...but ol' Frank was lucky that day. As he was fallin' to the ground he got off a lucky shot that hit Shorty in the chest. Shorty fell dead in his tracks an' that's how Morgan started his reputation. I was there an' I saw the whole thing."

Pettigrew was writing furiously to keep up with Ford's wild tale.

"So that's what started Frank's rep as a gunfighter," Ford went on. "He shot a man whose aim was bad. But Frank was slow, too damn slow to keep that slug from going through his right shoulder."

"My goodness," Pettigrew exclaimed. "It would appear that Mr. Morgan is something of a fraud...he *was* something of a fraud if, as you say, he's dead."

"He's damn sure dead," Vic said, draining his own glass of whiskey. "If you'll buy us another round of drinks, Mr. Pettigrew, I'll tell you what I know about Frank Morgan."

The writer's drink came to the table just as Vic was saying this. Pettigrew looked up from his notepad.

"Bring these gentlemen another round," he said.

Vic planned to invent his own story about Morgan, something that would keep the Easterner buying whiskey well into the night.

"You also knew Morgan?" Pettigrew asked.

"Not as well as Ford, but I saw him go up against this paid shootest down in Abilene. I'll tell you about it, soon as I'm done quenching my thirst."

Twenty-four

"I know it's you, Morgan! If you fire one more shot, I'll blow the kid's goddamn skull all over Lost Pine Canyon and leave him for the wolves!"

Pine edged out the front door of the cabin with his pistol under Conrad's chin.

"My men are gonna saddle our horses!" Pine went on with a fistful of Conrad's hair in his left hand. "One more gunshot and I blow your son's head off!"

Only silence filled the canyon after the echo of Ned's voice died.

"You hear me, Morgan?"

More silence, only the whisper of snow falling on ponderosa pine limbs.

"Answer me, you son of a bitch!"

The quiet around Ned was absolute. He squirmed a little, but he held his Colt under Conrad's jawbone with the hammer cocked.

"I'll kill this wimpy little bastard!" Ned warned what seemed like an empty forest.

And still, there was no reply from Morgan.

"Whoever you've got shootin' from up on the

rim, you'd best tell that son of a bitch I mean business. If he fires one shot I'll kill your boy."

Conrad Browning had tears streaming down his pale face and his legs were trembling. A dark purple bruise decorated one of his cheeks.

Ned looked over his shoulder at the cabin door. He spoke to Slade and Lyle. "You and Rich and Cabot get out there and saddle the best horses," he snapped. "Tell Billy Miller to keep his gun sights on the back."

"He ain't gonna shoot us?" Slade asked.

"Hell, no, he ain't," Pine replied.

"What makes you so all-fired sure?"

"Because I've got a gun at his boy's throat. He came all this way to save him. Morgan knows that even if he shoots me, I'll kill this kid as I'm going down. Now get those goddamn horses saddled."

"I see somebody up top!" cried Billy Miller, a boy from Nebraska who had killed a storekeeper to get a few plugs of tobacco.

"Kill the son of a bitch!" Ned shouted.

"He's gone now, but I seen him."

"Damn," Ned hissed, his jaw set. He spoke to Slade and Lyle again. "Get out there and put saddles on the best animals we've got. Hurry!"

"I ain't so sure about this, Ned," Lyle said, peering out the doorway.

"Get out there and saddle the goddamn horses or I'll kill you myself!" Ned cried. "Morgan ain't gonna do a damn thing so long as I've got this gun cocked under his little boy's skull bone."

Rich Boggs, a half-breed holdup man from Kansas, came out the front door carrying a rifle. "C'mon, boys," he said in a quiet voice.

Lyle and Slade edged out the door with Winchesters in their hands.

"I don't like this, Lyle," Slade said.

"Neither do I, Slade, but we can't stay here until this snow melts."

Cabot Bulware, a former bank robber from Baton Rouge, was the last to leave the cabin. He spoke Cajun English. "Don't see no mens no place, *mon ami*," he whispered. "Dis man Morgan be a hard *batard* to shoot."

"Shut up and get the damn horses saddled," Ned said, his hands trembling in the cold.

"Please don't shoot me, Mr. Pine," Conrad whimpered. "I didn't do anything to you."

"Shut up, boy, or I'll empty your brains onto this here snow," Ned spat. "I ain't all that sure you've got any goddamn brains."

"My father doesn't care what you do to me," Conrad said. "He never came to see me, not even when you killed my mother, Vivian."

"That was an accident, sort of. Now shut up and let me think."

Cabot, Lyle, Slade, and Billy made their way slowly to the corrals. Rich came over to Ned with his rifle cocked, ready to fire.

"You reckon Morgan will let us ride out of here?" Rich asked.

"Damn right he will."

"You sound mighty sure of it."

"I've got his snot-nosed kid with a gun under his jawbone. Even Morgan won't take the chance of shootin' at us. He knows I'll kill his boy."

"I ain't seen him no place, Ned. I've been looking real close."

"Help the others saddle our mounts. Frank Morgan is out there somewhere."

"Are you sure it's him? Billy saw a feller up on the rim of the canyon. Maybe it's the law."

"It ain't the law. It's Morgan."

"But you sent Charlie back to gun him down, an' then Sam and Buster and Tony rode our back trail. One man couldn't outgun Sam or Buster, and nobody's ever gotten to Charlie. Charlie's real careful."

"Shut the hell up and help saddle our horses, Rich. You're wasting valuable time running your mouth over things we can't do nothing about. If Morgan got to Charlie and Sam and the rest of them, we'll have to ride out of here and head for Gypsum Gap to meet up with Vic."

"One man can't be that tough," Rich said, although he made for the corrals as he said it.

Ned was furious. He'd known Morgan was good, but that was years ago.

He stood in front of the cabin with his Colt pistol under Conrad's chin, waiting for the horses. At the moment he needed a swallow of whiskey.

Louis Pettigrew had begun to have serious doubts. He'd been listening to Victor Vanbergen and Ford Peters talk about Frank Morgan for more than an hour. Louis had a page full of notes on Morgan.

But too many seasoned lawmen had told him that Morgan was as good as any man alive with a gun. Something about the stories he was hearing didn't add up.

"Morgan left his wife with a band of outlaws?" Louis asked with disbelief. "And they killed her?"

"Sure did," Vic said.

"That ain't the worst of it," Ford added. "She had this baby boy of Frank's. He left the kid with her too. That oughta tell you what kind of yellow bastard he is...he was, until he got killed. The little boy's name was Conrad Browning. Morgan wasn't even decent enough to marry her before he pulled stakes and ran out on her."

"Did Mr. Morgan ever come back to visit his son?" Louis asked.

"Not that anybody knows of. The boy was raised by somebody else. Morgan was rotten through an' through. Any man who'd abandon his own son ain't worth the gunpowder it'd take to kill him, if you ask me."

Vic nodded. "That's a fact. Morgan went west and left his boy to grow up alone. That's why we say he was yellow. No man with even a trace of gumption would leave his kid to be raised by somebody else."

"Morgan was a no-good son of a bitch," Ford said, waving to the barkeep to bring them more drinks at the expense of the writer from Boston.

"I can't believe he'd do that," Louis said, turning the page on his notepad.

"You didn't know him like we did," Ford said. "He was trash."

"I don't understand how so many people could be wrong about him," Louis said. "I've heard him described as fearless, and one of the best gunmen in recent times."

"Lies," Vic said. "All lies."

"He was short on nerve," Ford added as more shot glasses of whiskey came toward their table. "I can tell you a helluva lot more about him, if you want to hear it."

The drinks were placed around the table. Louis Pettigrew had a scowl on his face.

"I don't think I need to hear any more, gentlemen. It would appear I've come all this way for nothing...to write a story about a dead gunfighter who had a reputation he clearly did not deserve."

"You've got that part right," Vic said.

Ford nodded his agreement.

Vern wanted to get in his two cents' worth. "Frank Morgan is washed up as a gunfighter. You'd better write your story about somebody else."

"Dear me," Pettigrew said, closing his notepad, putting his pencil away. "It would seem the last of the great gunfighters is no more."

A blast of cold wind rattled the doors into the Wagon Wheel Saloon. Pettigrew glanced over his shoulder. "I suppose I should see about lodging for the night, and a stable for my horse. I think in the morning I'll ride toward Denver and catch the next train to Boston."

"Sounds like a good idea to me," Vic said. "You won't be givin' your readers much if you write a story about Frank Morgan."

"So it would appear, gentlemen. I appreciate your time and your honesty. I suppose some men live on reputations from the past."

"That's Morgan," Ford said. "I hate to inform a feller that he's wasted his time, but I figure you have if you intend to write about Frank."

Pettigrew pushed back his chair. "So many people want to read the dime novels about true-life heroes out here in the West. Some of our best-selling books in the past have been about Wild Bill and Buffalo Bill Cody. There's even this woman, Calamity Jane they call her, who can outshoot most men with a rifle or a pistol. Our readers love this sort of thing. We can't print enough of them."

"Nobody'd want to read about Frank," Vic said. "It'd be a waste of good paper and ink."

Pettigrew had gone outside before Ford and Vic began to laugh over their joke.

"You spooned him full of crap," Vern said, grinning. "He bought every word of it."

Vic's expression changed. "We don't need some damn reporter hangin' around while Ned's got Frank's boy."

"We got rid of the reporter," Ford said. "I figure he'll head for Denver at first light."

"If this storm don't snow him in," Vern observed, watching snowflakes patter against the saloon windows. "That's one helluva long ride up to Denver when the weather's as bad as this."

"We'll stay here tonight," Vic said. "Go tell the rest of the boys to find rooms and put their horses away."

Vern stood up, stretching tired muscles after the ride from Gypsum Gap. "I'm damn sure glad to hear you say that, Boss," he said.

"Me too," Ford agreed. "Our asses could have froze off. It sure is late in the year for so much snow."

Vic looked out at the storm. "We need to send a couple of riders down to Pine Canyon," he said, "just to make sure Ned got Morgan and that boy."

"We'd have heard by now," Ford observed.

"Somebody from Ned's bunch would have come lookin' for us if they needed help," Vern said. "Hell, Morgan's just one man an' Ned's got over a dozen good gunmen with him. Slade an' Lyle are enough to drop Morgan in his tracks."

"I hope you're right," Vic said. "Morgan can be a sneaky son of a bitch."

"He ain't *that* sneaky," Ford said.

Vic glanced at Ford and smiled. "How the hell would you know, Ford? In spite of what you told that Easterner, you've never set eyes on Frank Morgan in your life. He could walk in here right now and you wouldn't recognize him."

Ford chuckled. "You're right about that, Boss. I just couldn't pass up the opportunity."

Vern started for the door, sleeving into his coat as he passed the potbelly stove. "You damn sure did a good job of it, Ford Peters. For a while there, I thought maybe you an' Frank was half brothers."

"I'd kill you over a remark like that," Ford said, "if it wasn't so damn cold."

Vic tossed back the last of his third drink. "Tell the boys to settle in for the night, Vern. I'll send a couple of 'em over to the canyon tomorrow, so we'll know what's keepin' Ned. I had it figured he oughta be here by now."

Twenty-five

Frank watched from hiding as Ned Pine brought Conrad out of the cabin with a gun under his chin. The boy's hands were tied in front of him. Swirling snow kept Frank from seeing the boy clearly.

Five more members of the gang brought seven saddled horses around to the front. Frank was helpless. For now, all he could do was watch.

He wondered if Pine would execute his son for the men he'd already lost. But Pine needed a human shield to get him out of the box canyon. He needed Conrad alive. For now.

"Pine will kill Conrad when he hears the first gunshot," Frank whispered. "I'll have to follow them, and wait until Ned makes a mistake."

He wondered where they were taking his son. Frank had taken a deadly toll on Pine's gang in a matter of hours, with the help of the old fur trapper.

Frank felt something touch his shoulder, and he whirled around, snaking a pistol from leather. He relaxed and put his Peacemaker away.

"Don't shoot me," Tin Pan Rushing said softly. "They're clearin' out, as you can see."

"I've got no choice but to trail them. Maybe Ned will get careless somewhere."

"Where will they take him?"

"I've got no idea, but wherever it is, I'll be right behind them. I don't know this country."

"I do," Tin Pan said. "Been here for nigh onto twenty years."

"This isn't your problem. I appreciate what you've done for me, but I can handle it from here."

"I'll fetch one of them dead outlaw's horses from behind the canyon. I'll ride with you."

"No need, Tin Pan. This isn't your fight."

"I decided to make it my fight, Morgan. When some ornery bastards are holdin' a man's son hostage, he needs all the help he can get."

"That was a nice shot from up high a while ago. Couldn't have done any better myself."

"I was hopin' the wind didn't throw my aim off. But this ol' long gun is pretty damn accurate. I'll collect that horse and unsaddle the others so I can let 'em go. I'll bring your animals around, along with Martha, to the mouth of the canyon soon as they ride out."

"I'd almost forgotten about your mule."

"She's got more'n fifty cured beaver pelts tied to her back, and that's a plenty to get me a fresh grubstake before the weather gets warm and the beaver start to lose their winter hair. You might say that's a winter's worth of work hangin' across her packsaddle."

"Here they come," Frank said, peering into the snow. "Stay still."

"No need for you to tell me what to do, Morgan. I know how to make it in this wilderness without being seen. Rest easy on that notion."

Ned Pine rode at the front with Conrad, Pine's gun still pressed to Conrad's throat. Two more gunmen rode behind Ned and the boy. A third outlaw came from the cabin leading a loaded packhorse.

The last pair of outlaws stayed well behind the others with Winchester rifles resting on their thighs.

"Keepin' back a rear guard," Tin Pan observed. "If we get the chance, we might be able to jump 'em in this snow. It's hard to see real well."

"I was thinking the same thing," Frank said. "One way or another, I've got to get rid of Pine's men before I take him on man-to-man."

"You'll need to pick the right spot and the right time," Tin Pan reminded him.

"I'm a pretty good hand at that," Frank told him, moving back into the trees as Pine and his men rode out of the canyon with Conrad as their prisoner.

Snowflakes swirled around the men as they left the canyon and turned east, away from the badlands. Frank was surprised at the direction they took.

Barnaby Jones parked his rented buggy in Cortez. His drive down from Denver had been brutal and he was sure he'd almost frozen to death. Had it not been for three bottles of imported French sherry, he was certain he wouldn't have made it through this wilderness in a blizzard.

He stopped in front of the sheriff's office and took a wool blanket off his lap before he climbed down from the seat. He removed his gloves. Cortez was a mere spot in the road, a dot on the map he bought in Denver after he got off the train.

"The things I do to get a story," he mumbled, wondering if his editor at *Harper's Magazine* would appreciate the difficulty he'd gone through.

He entered the sheriff's door without knocking, enjoying the warmth from a cast-iron stove in a corner of the tiny room. A jail cell sat at the back of the place.

A man with a gray handlebar mustache

looked up at him with a question on his face. He was seated at a battered rolltop desk with a newspaper in his lap.

"Sheriff Jim Sikes?" Barnaby asked.

"That's me." The lawman looked him up and down. "Stranger, you ain't dressed for this climate. Didn't anybody tell you it gets cold in Colorado Territory?"

"Yessiree, they did," Barnaby replied, offering his hand. "I am Barnaby Jones from *Harper's Magazine* in New York. I'm wearing long underwear under my suit."

"What brings you to Cortez?" the sheriff asked.

Barnaby pulled off his bowler hat. "The United States marshal in Denver told me to look you up. I'm writing a story for my magazine about a retired gunfighter named Frank Morgan, and Marshal Williams said you would know if he's in this part of the country. One of our competitors, the *Boston Globe*, has sent a reporter out here to interview this Mr. Morgan. I'd like to talk to Morgan myself."

"He ain't in these parts, mister. Marshal Williams is wrong about that. If Morgan was around, I'd know about it. I'd have dead men stacked up here like cordwood."

Barnaby edged over to the stove, warming his backside as best he could. "I have other information. A writer by the name of Louis Pettigrew from the *Globe* found out that Morgan is in southwestern Colorado. I'm only a day or two behind Mr. Pettigrew."

"You're both wrong."

"How can you be so sure, Sheriff?"

"Like I said, no dead bodies. Maybe you ought to have the wax cleaned out of your ears. I said it real plain the first time."

"But I *know* he's somewhere close by. Pettigrew left the day before I did. He rented a horse in Denver and came down here. Something about Morgan's son being a prisoner of some outlaw gang."

"We've got a few outlaws," Sheriff Sikes said. "Some of 'em are in town right now. Victor Vanbergen and his bunch of toughs are down at the Wagon Wheel, but they haven't caused any trouble. I think they're just passing through."

"I never heard of Victor Vanbergen. Who is he?"

"A bank robber. A thief and a killer. But so long as he don't cause no trouble in my town, I'm leaving him and his boys alone."

Barnaby reached inside his heavy wool coat, taking out a few papers. "Who is Ned Pine?"

"A hired gun. Worse than Vanbergen. He heads up one of the old outlaw gangs in this part of the West, but the last I heard of him he was down south. Texas, I think."

"Mr. Pettigrew of the *Boston Globe* believes he's here, and that he has Frank Morgan's son as a hostage."

"It's news to me," Sheriff Sikes remarked. "I'd have had something over the telegraph wire by now if Ned Pine and his men were close by."

Barnaby shook his head. "I still think I have good information about Pine. And Morgan."

Sikes went back to reading his paper. "You're welcome to look around Cortez," he said, a hint of impatience in his hoarse voice. "But Morgan ain't here, and neither is Pine. Van-bergen just showed up today. I judge he'll be gone by tomorrow if this snow lets up."

"Where can I hire a room for the night?" Barnaby asked. "And I need a place to stable my buggy horse."

"Ain't but one hotel in town, the Cortez Hotel. It's just down the street. You can't miss it."

"Have I come too late to buy dinner?"

"Mary over at the cafe might have some stew left. She's about to close, so I'd hurry if I was you."

"Thank you, Sheriff. I'm thankful for the information you gave me."

"You're wasting your time in Cortez looking for Ned Pine or Frank Morgan. We don't get many of the real bad hard cases in this town. They usually pass right on through, if the weather's decent."

Barnaby put on his hat and walked out the door. The wind had picked up after sun-down, and bits of ice and snow stung his cheeks as he climbed back in his snow-covered buggy.

Frank sat his horse, watching Ned Pine and his men ride across a snow-covered valley.

"He's got those two men covering the back trail," he said to Tin Pan.

"This snow is mighty heavy, Morgan," Tin Pan said. "If we ride around 'em and cut off those two gunslingers, we can put 'em in the ground."

"They're keeping about a quarter mile between them and Ned," Frank said. "If this snow keeps up, Ned won't notice if I jump in front of them and have them toss down their guns."

"You ain't gonna kill 'em?"

"Not unless they don't give me a choice."

"What the hell are you gonna do? Tie the both of them to a tree?"

"I'll show you, if they'll allow it. Follow me and we'll cut them off."

Rich Boggs was shivering, nursing a pint of whiskey in the icy wind. "To hell with this, Cabot," he said. "We're not making a dime messing around with Frank Morgan's kid. I say we cut out of here and head south."

"Ned would follow us and kill us," Cabot Bulware replied with a woolen shawl covering his mouth. "This is a personal thing for Ned."

"I'm freezin' to death," Rich said.

"So am I," Cabot replied. "I'm from Baton Rouge. I'm not used to this cold, *mon ami*."

"To hell with it then," Rich remarked. "When Ned and Lyle and Slade and Billy ride over that next ridge, let's get the hell out of here."

"I am afraid of Ned," Cabot replied. "I do not want to die out here in this snow."

Rich stood up suddenly in his stirrups and pulled his sorrel to a halt. "Who the hell is that with the rifle pointed straight at us?" he asked Cabot.

"There are two of them," Cabot replied. "There is another one on foot standing behind that tree, and he also has a rifle aimed at us."

"Damn!" Rich exclaimed, ready to open his coat and reach for his pistol.

"Climb down, boys," a deep voice demanded. "Keep your hands up where I can see them."

"Morgan," Cabot whispered, although he followed the instructions he'd been given.

"Step away from your horses!"

They did as they were told. Rich could feel the small hairs rising on the back of his neck.

"Take your pistols out and toss 'em down!" another voice said from behind a tree trunk.

Rich threw his Colt .44 into the snow.

Cabot opened his mackinaw carefully and dropped his Smith and Wesson .45 near his feet.

"Get their horses and guns, Tin Pan," the man holding the rifle said. "I'll keep 'em covered."

An old man in a coonskin cap came toward them carrying a large-bore rifle. He picked up their pistols and took their horses' reins, leading them off the trail.

"All right, boys," the rifleman in front of them said. "I've got one more thing for you to do."

"What the hell is that, mister?" Rich snapped, giving Cabot a quick glance.

"Sit down right where you are and pull off your boots."

"What?"

"Pull off your damn boots."

"But our feet'll freeze. We'll get the frostbite."

"Would you rather be dead?"

"No," Cabot said softly, sitting down in the snow to pull off his boots.

"We'll die out here without no boots!" Rich complained. "We can't make it in our stocking feet."

"I can shoot you now," the rifleman said. "That way, your feet won't be cold."

Rich slumped to his rump and pulled off his stovepipe boots without further complaint.

"Now start walking," the rifleman said. "I don't give a damn which direction you go."

"We will die!" Cabot cried.

The lanky gunman came toward them and picked up their boots without taking his rifle sights off them. "Life ain't no easy proposition, gentlemen," he said. "Start walking, or I'll kill you right where you sit."

Twenty-six

Darkness came to the snow-clad mountains. Rich Boggs was hobbling toward the cabin at Lost Pine Canyon on seriously frostbitten feet. Cabot Bulware was behind him, using a pine limb for a crutch.

"It ain't much farther," Rich groaned. "I can see the mouth of the canyon from here."

"*Sacré*," Cabot said, limping with most of his weight on the crutch. "I be gon' kill that *batard* Morgan if I can get my hands on a horse and a gun."

"I just wanna get my feet warm," Rich said. "The way I feel now, I ain't interested in killin' nobody. I think a couple of my toes fell off."

"Who was the old man with Monsieur Morgan?" Cabot asked. "I hear Ned say Morgan always work alone."

"Don't know," Rich replied, his teeth chattering from the numbing cold. "Just some old son of a bitch in a coonskin cap with a rifle."

"He be dangerous too," Cabot warned. "I see the look in his eyes."

"You're too goddamn superstitious, Cabot. He'll die just like any other man if you shoot him in the right place. I can guarantee it."

"My feet are frozen. I go back to Baton Rouge when I can find a horse. I don't like this place."

"I ain't all that fond of it either, Cabot," Rich said as they moved slowly to the canyon entrance. "It was a big mistake to side with Ned on this thing. I never did see how we was gonna make any money."

"I do not care about money now," Cabot replied. "All I want is a stove where I can warm my feet."

"Won't be but another half mile to the cabin," Rich told him in a shivering voice. "All we've gotta do is get there before our feet freeze off.

"Boots and horses are what we need," Rich continued. "If they didn't leave our horses in the corral, we're a couple of dead men in this weather."

"I feel dead now," Cabot replied. "I don't got feeling at all in either one of my feet."

As night blanketed the canyon Rich added more wood to the stove. He and Cabot had dragged the dead bodies outside, but a broken window let in so much cold air that Rich was still shivering. He'd taken the boots off Don Jones's body and forced his feet into them. Cabot was wearing boots and an extra pair of socks that once belonged to Mack.

They'd found two pistols and a small amount of ammunition among the dead men. Ned and the others had taken all the food. Thus Rich was boiling fistfuls of snow in an old coffeepot full of yesterday's grounds.

Five horses were still in the corral, even though the gate was open. They were nibbling from the stack of hay. Thus, there were enough saddles to go around.

"I am going back south in the morning," Cabot said with his palms open near the stove.

"Me too," Rich said. "I'm finished with Ned and this bunch of bullshit over gettin' even with Frank Morgan. There's no payday in it for us."

"I've been dreaming about a bowl of hot crawfish gumbo and hush puppies all afternoon," Cabot said wistfully. "This is not where I belong."

"Me either. I'm headed down to Mexico, where it's warm all the time."

Cabot turned to the broken window where Don had been shot in the face. "What was that noise?" he asked.

"I didn't hear no noise," Rich replied.

"One of the horses in the corral...it snorted, or made some kind of sound."

"My ears are so damn cold I couldn't hear a thing nohow," Rich declared. "Maybe it was just your imagination. All I hear is snow fallin' on this roof."

Then Cabot heard it again.

"Help...me!" a faint voice cried.

"That sounded like Jerry's voice," Cabot said, jumping up with a pistol in his fist.

"I heard it that time," Rich said, getting up with Mack's gun to open the door a crack.

Rich saw a sight he would remember for the rest of his life. Jerry Page came crawling toward them on his hands and knees in the snow, leaving a trail of blood behind him.

Rich and Cabot rushed outside to help him.

"Morgan," Jerry gasped. "Morgan came up on the rim and stuck a knife in me. He killed...Roger. Cut his throat with the same Bowie knife."

"We'll take you in by the fire," Cabot said as he took one of Jerry's shoulders.

"I'm froze stiff," Jerry complained, trembling from weakness and cold. "I'm bleedin' real bad. You gotta get me to a doctor real quick."

"We can't go nowhere in this snowstorm," Rich said as they helped the wounded man into the cabin. "It'll have to wait for morning."

"I'm dyin'," Jerry croaked. "You gotta help me. Where's Ned?"

"Ned and the others pulled out. We ran into Morgan too. He took our boots and guns and horses. We damn near froze to death gettin' back here."

They placed Jerry on a blanket beside the stove and covered him with a moth-eaten patchwork quilt.

"Morgan," Jerry stuttered. "He ain't human. He's like a mountain lion. Me an' Roger never heard a thing until he was on top of us."

"We figured there was trouble when neither one of you came back," Rich said bitterly. "Morgan killed most of the others. Only Lyle, Slade, Billy, and Ned made it out of here alive."

"What happened...to Morgan's kid?"

"Ned had a gun to his head," Rich recalled.

"That's the...only way it's gonna stop," Jerry moaned as he put a hand over the deep knife wound between his ribs. "Ned's gotta let that boy go."

"Ned's gone crazy for revenge. He won't stop until he kills Morgan."

"Morgan...will...kill him first," Jerry assured them. "I need a drink of whiskey. Anything."

"We're boilin' old coffee grounds," Rich said. "There ain't no whiskey. Ned and the others took it all with them when we pulled out of here."

"Water," Jerry whispered, his ice-clad eyelids fluttering as if he was losing consciousness. "Gimme some water. Morgan's gonna kill us all unless Ned...lets that boy go."

"You know Ned," Cabot said, pouring a cup of weak coffee for Jerry, steaming rising from a rusted tin cup. "He won't listen to reason."

"I'm gonna die...way up here in Colorado," Jerry said as his eyes closed. "I sure as hell wish I was home where I could see my mama one more time..."

Jerry's chest stopped moving.

"Don't waste that coffee," Rich said. "Jerry's on his way back home now."

Cabot stared into the cup. "This is not coffee, *mon ami*. It is only warm water with a little color in it."

Ned paced back and forth as a fire burned under a rocky ledge in the bend of a dry streambed.

"Where the hell is Rich and Cabot?" he asked, glancing once at Conrad, bound hand and foot beneath the outcrop where the fire flickered. It was dark, and still snowing, though the snowfall had let up some.

"They ain't comin'," Lyle said.

"What the hell do you mean, they ain't coming?" Ned barked with his jaw set hard.

"Morgan got to 'em," Slade said from his lookout point on top of the ledge. "They'd have been here by now, if they were able."

"Slade's right," Billy said, with his Winchester resting on his shoulder. "Some way or other, Frank Morgan slipped up behind 'em and got 'em both."

"Bullshit!" Ned cried. "Morgan is an old man, a has-been in the gunman's trade. He doesn't have it in him to slip up behind Rich and Cabot."

"I figure he got Jerry and Roger," Slade went on without raising his voice. "We know he shot all those others back at the cabin. Then you've got to wonder what happened to Sam and Buster and Tony back on the trail when they went to check on Charlie."

Lyle grunted. "Morgan must be slick," he said, casting a wary glance around their camp. "I wish we'd never gotten into this mess. That kid over yonder ain't worth no million dollars to nobody."

"He ain't worth a plug nickel to me," Billy Miller said as he added wood to the fire. "I say we kill the little bastard an' get clear of this cold country."

Ned turned on his men. "We're not leaving until Frank Morgan is dead!" he yelled.

Lyle gave Ned a look. "Who's gonna kill him, Ned? We ain't had much luck tryin' it so far."

"We'll join up with Victor at Gypsum Gap and hunt him down like a dog," Ned replied.

Slade shrugged. "Bein' outnumbered don't seem to bother Morgan all that much."

"Are you taking Morgan's side?" Ned asked.

"I'm not takin' any side but my own. My main purpose now is to stay alive."

"Me too," Billy added.

"Same goes for me," Lyle muttered. "This Morgan feller is a handful."

"Are you boys yellow?" Ned demanded.

"Nope," Lyle was the first to say. "Just smart. If a man is a man-hunter by profession, he's usually mighty damn good at it if he lives very long."

"I never met a man who didn't make a mistake," Ned said, coming back to the fire to warm his hands.

"So far," Slade said quietly, "Morgan hasn't made very many."

"One of you saddle a horse and ride back down the trail to see if you can find Rich and Cabot," Ned ordered, his patience worn thin.

"I'm not going," Slade said. "That's exactly what a man like Morgan will want us to do."

"What the hell do you mean?" Ned inquired, knocking snowflakes from the brim of his hat.

"He wants us to split up, so he can take us down a few at a time."

"Slade's right," Lyle said.

"We oughta stay together," Billy chimed in. "At least until we join up with Vic an' his boys."

"Morgan!" Ned spat, pacing again. "That son of a bitch is a dead man when I get him in my sights."

"That'll be the problem," Lyle offered. "A man like Morgan don't let you get him in your gun sights all that often, an' when he does, there's usually a reason."

"He'll come after us tonight," Billy said,

glancing around at forest shadows. "He's liable to kill us in our bedrolls if we ain't careful."

"I'm not goin' to sleep tonight," Slade said.

"Why's that?" Ned asked.

Slade grinned. "I want to make damn sure I see the sun come up tomorrow mornin'."

Ned was fuming now. Even his two best gunmen, Lyle and Slade, showed signs of fear.

"You ride back a ways, Billy," Ned said. "Just a mile or two."

"I won't do it, Ned."

"Are you disobeying a direct order from me?" Ned demanded as he opened his coat.

"Yessir, I am," Billy replied. "If Morgan's back there, he'll kill me from ambush."

Ned snaked his Colt from a holster. He aimed for Billy's stomach. "Get on one of those horses and ride southwest to see if you can find Rich and Cabot. If you don't, I'll damn sure kill you myself."

Billy Miller's eyes rounded. "You'd shoot me down for not goin' back?"

"I damn sure will. Get mounted."

Billy backed away from the fire with his palms spread wide. "You let this Morgan feller get stuck in your craw, Ned. I never seen you like this."

"Get on that goddamn horse. See if you can find their tracks."

Billy turned his back on Ned and trudged off to the picket ropes.

"You may have just gotten that boy killed," Slade said tonelessly.

Twenty-seven

Billy hunched his shoulders into the wind, buttoning his coat underneath his chin. He wore thin leather gloves that did little to keep out the cold.

"Ned's tryin' to get me killed," he mumbled, gripping the Winchester resting across the pommel of his saddle as the brown gelding plodded into sheets of tiny snowflakes. Billy knew Lyle and Slade were too smart to ride their back trail in the dark with Frank Morgan behind them.

So much snow had fallen since they made camp under the rock ledge that Billy couldn't find their own tracks, much less those of Rich and Cabot...or Frank Morgan's.

"He'll shoot me right out of the saddle," Billy told himself in a whisper, searching both sides of a narrow mining road leading west, flanked by tall pines. They had ridden this road in daylight and now it was pitch dark, a condition made worse by the snow.

I'm a dead man, Billy thought, shuddering when a blast of cold wind came toward him.

But he was just as dead if Ned Pine shot him for refusing to look for Rich and Cabot.

His gelding pricked up its ears, watching something ahead of him on the trail.

"It's Morgan," Billy said, pulling back on the reins to study the situation. "Don't nothing hurt no worse than being shot when it's cold," he mumbled.

A bounty hunter had put a bullet through his leg one winter as Billy was leaving Amarillo with twenty head of stolen cows, and nothing, not even his dad's woodshed whippings when he was a kid, had hurt any worse.

I won't do this, Billy thought.

He reined his horse off the road into the ponderosa pines and waited.

"Just one of 'em," Tin Pan whispered. "His horse caught our scent 'cause we is upwind."

Frank jacked a shell into the firing chamber of his Winchester. "I'll go after him on foot," he said. "Keep an eye out, in case the rest of them are close by."

"You're wastin' good wind," Tin Pan told him. "I always keep an eye on things. Martha will tell me if they get round behind us."

Frank crept off into the darkness, making a wide sweep to get behind the rider they'd seen.

"He's a worrier," Tin Pan said to himself. "What he needs is a really good mountain mule."

Billy swung down from the saddle and tied his horse off to a pine limb.

"I'll just sit here and wait for half an hour," he said to no one in particular. "Ned won't know the difference if I tell him I couldn't find any tracks."

He hunkered down behind a ponderosa trunk to be out of the wind, cradling his Winchester next to his chest while he searched the black forest around him, his teeth chattering.

"I'm gonna quit this outfit," he promised himself, thinking about home. And being warm.

"I can kill you now," a soft voice said behind him.

Billy jerked his head around.

"Who's there?" he asked, bringing the muzzle of his rifle up quickly.

"Lay that Winchester down or I'll put a tunnel through your head," the voice said.

"It's you, Morgan!"

"That's right."

"How did you get behind me?"

"Quietly."

"Ain't nobody can be that quiet," Billy said.

"I'll only tell you one more time to drop that rifle."

Billy let the Winchester slide from his hands into the snow at his feet.

"That's better. Where's Ned? And my son?"

"East. Maybe two miles. Please don't kill me, Mr. Morgan. I didn't want no part of this right from the start. It was Ned's idea. He's taking your boy up to Gypsum Gap to meet up with Vic Vanbergen."

"I can't leave you alive. You'll go back and join forces with Ned Pine again."

"No, sir, I won't. I swear it."

"Only one way to be sure."

"Are you gonna kill me?"

"Take your pistol out of the holster and throw it as far as you can in my direction."

"Yessir," Billy stammered, reaching into his coat very slowly to take out his Colt .44. He tossed it toward the voice.

"Now take off your boots."

"My boots?"

"That's what I said. Pull 'em off."

"My feet are gonna freeze off."

"Would you rather be dead?"

"No, sir."

"Then take 'em off."

"I got holes in my socks. My big toe is stickin' through the left one."

"You can hop back to camp on your right foot. Pull the boots off."

Billy reached for his right boot. "Are you gonna leave me my horse?"

"Hadn't planned on it."

"But I'll freeze to death."

"I can kill you right now and that won't be a worry," the voice said. "Is that what you want?"

"No, sir, I'm takin' my boots off now. Just please don't shoot me. I told you the truth. Ned's headed for Gypsum Gap to join up with Vic."

Louis Pettigrew set off before dawn to ride for Denver. He had no story to write. Frank Morgan wasn't the legend people thought he was.

His ride back to Denver would take two days, and in a snowstorm like this he would suffer, unless he could find food and lodging.

228

He carried strips of jerky and tins of peaches in his saddlebags. And a bottle of whiskey.

"What a waste," Louis told himself, snuggling inside his coat with a wool muffler wrapped around his face. His nose had no feeling in it.

If time allowed he would stop off in Abilene, Kansas, to inquire as to the whereabouts of Wyatt Earp. Word was that he had already moved south to Tucson, leaving Louis with no one to write about.

Odd about Morgan, he thought. So many lawmen had said that Frank Morgan was the last of the true gunfighters roaming the West.

"Wonder how so many could be wrong," he said, guiding his horse down an empty, snow-covered stretch of road that would take him to Denver...if he didn't freeze to death.

"The things a writer will do for a story," he mumbled between numb lips. It would be a couple of hours until dawn brought warmer weather.

The road he had taken would pass through a place called Gypsum Gap, an abandoned mining town north of Cortez that had been a big gold-mining area.

Vic sat up in bed. He reached for the washstand beside his bed and checked his pocket watch for the hour.

"Five o'clock," he grumbled, tossing aside the quilts on his bed at the Cortez Hotel. "Time we got saddled and headed back to the Gap."

He dressed quickly, for the tiny room had no heat and he was cold. When he was fully attired, he walked into the hallway and knocked on Ford Peters's door.

"Who is it?"

"Vic. Get the rest of the boys up."

"What the hell time is it?" Ford asked sleepily.

"Time for you to get your ass out of bed. It's past five in the morning. We've got to get the hell out of here before Ned shows up at the Gap with that boy."

"It's too damn early," Ford said through the thin door leading into the hall.

"Get out of bed." Vic snapped. "Get the men on their horses and meet me in front of the hotel."

"Damn, damn, damn," Peters mumbled. Then Vic heard the squeak of bed springs.

Larry and Ashford rode out front, complaining about the hour and the cold.

"It's still snowin'," Larry said, shrouded in snowflakes as he urged his pinto forward.

"You've got real good eyes," Ashford told him, steering his horse around a deep snow-drift. "I'm real damn glad to hear that you don't need spectacles."

Vern rode up beside them, speaking in a low voice. "The boss don't like all this complaining. He threatened to kill Todd a minute ago on account of Todd said his feet was cold. I'd be real careful about the complaints."

"I've got a splittin' headache," Kirk Stearman said, his face a pale white.

"Too much whiskey last night," Vern remarked. "You shoulda gone to bed early."

"What the hell are we doin' up here?" Kirk asked. "This don't make no sense to me."

"Followin' orders," Vern grumbled.

"But how the hell are we gonna make any money off this kid Ned Pine has got?" Kirk was careful to keep his voice soft when he said it.

"Ask Vic," Ford said. "It's a question that might get you shot off your horse before daylight."

"It just don't make no sense." Kirk had a deep scowl on his face.

Ford glanced up at clouds heavy with more snow. "When you join a gang, you don't ask questions if things don't seem to make sense. You follow orders."

"Has anybody got any whiskey?" Kirk asked. "I need a little hair of the dog to cure what ails me."

"I drank all mine," Ford replied.

"Me too," Vern added, "but I sure as hell wish I'd saved a swallow or two."

Steve Bandas overheard what was being said as he tried to keep his dun gelding moving in the right direction. "Whiskey is what we all need," he said.

Tyler Feagin, a gunman from eastern Texas, spat loudly into the snow. "What we need is to get the hell back to where it's warm. It's colder'n hell up at that old mining town in Gypsum

Gap. The goddamn wind blows through every crack in that mining office."

"Shut up, Tyler," Vern said. "Vic's liable to be listening to every word you say."

"Right now, I don't give a damn. I never heard of this Frank Morgan. We ain't gonna split up no million dollars for helpin' Ned capture his boy."

"You gonna brace Vic with it?" Vern asked.

Ford gave Tyler a stare. "Speak up loud, Tyler. Are you gonna jump Ned and Vic over it?"

"Nope," Tyler said, dropping his head. "I'd aimed to stay alive."

"Now you're usin' your brain," Ford remarked, "You ain't no match for Ned or Vic."

Tyler glanced over his shoulder. "One of us could slip up behind Vic and blow his goddamn head off. That way, we could get out of this cold weather an' head south."

"You try it," Ford told him.

Vern nodded his agreement. "Yeah, Tyler. You ride up back of him and pull the trigger."

Tyler fell silent as the string of outlaws rode up a steepening trail into the mountains east of Cortez.

"Whiskey," Kirk muttered again. "All I need is a couple of swallows of whiskey."

The road made a bend. Ford Peters was riding out in front now.

"Frank Morgan," Vern complained. "I've never been so sick of hearin' one man's name in my life."

"He's bad news," Steve said.

"How can things be much worse than ridin' through a goddamn blizzard at six in the morning?"

"I should have taken that job at the post office down in Goliad," Steve said.

Skies to the east had begun to turn gray. Victor Vanbergen kept his gunmen moving toward Gypsum Gap in spite of the cold and snow, figuring that Ned Pine had something big up his sleeve.

Twenty-eight

Just as dawn lightened the sky, Lyle tensed on his perch on top of the ledge. He saw a man on foot limping toward them through deep snowdrifts.

"I think we're about to find out what happened to Billy," he said to Ned while Ned added wood to the fire. "It don't appear Cabot an' Rich are with him."

"Do you see Billy?" Lyle asked

"Billy ain't got no horse...if it's Billy," Slade said as he lowered his rifle

"No horse?" Ned asked, straightening up from nursing the flames under their coffeepot.

Slade shook his head. "Seems like Mr. Frank Morgan found Billy before Billy found Rich and Cabot. Or where Morgan left their bodies."

Lyle spoke again. "This Morgan feller must

be mighty good at stalking a man...even if he's older than dirt like you say, Ned."

"Son of a bitch," Ned muttered.

"Don't shoot!" a voice cried.

"That's Billy," Slade added tonelessly.

Billy Miller hobbled into camp with a slightly dazed look on his face. He was staggering, about to fall as he made his way toward the fire.

"Where the hell's your boots?" Lyle asked with a wry smile tugging at his mouth.

"Where's your horse?" Ned demanded.

"Morgan got 'em," Billy stammered, his teeth chattering. "He's right behind us. I gotta warm my feet at that fire while I tell you about it. I can't feel my own damn feet. They's froze."

Billy stumbled toward the fire below the outcrop and fell down on his rump, placing his stocking feet close to the flames for a moment.

"How the hell did Morgan get the jump on you?" Ned wanted to know, the harsh tone of his voice betraying his rage as he questioned Billy.

Billy closed his eyes. "I was ridin' down our back trail. I stopped to look at some hoofprints. Morgan was hidin' in the dark off to one side of the road. He told me to throw down my guns or he'd kill me."

"You gave up without a fight?" Ned snapped.

"He had me cold, Boss. Wasn't anything else I could do right then."

"What did he say?" Ned asked.

"He wanted to know about his boy, and where we was takin' him."

"Did you tell Morgan we were headed up to Gypsum Gap?"

"I only said we was ridin' north. He said he knew that already."

"You're a damn fool and a yellow son of a bitch," Ned spat, reaching inside his coat for his pistol. "I won't have a man like your ridin' in my gang."

Billy stared into the muzzle of Ned's Colt. "You ain't gonna shoot me, are you?"

Ned thumbed back the hammer on his revolver.

"Don't do it, Ned," Lyle said softly. "We may need every man we've got."

"Billy Miller ain't a man," Ned replied, jutting his square jaw.

"Morgan's liable to hear the gunshot," Slade warned with a glance over his shoulder.

"I don't give a damn," Ned told him. "This idiot already told Morgan where we are."

An explosion echoed from the dry streambed when Ned's gun went off.

Billy was slammed to the ground with a dark hole near his right temple. Blood began squirting from the wound, covering the snow around his head.

Conrad Browning started to gag. He rolled over on his side and vomited.

Billy's legs began to twitch. His eyes were tightly shut as a groan escaped his lips.

"Billy won't be needin' no boots now," Lyle observed dryly. "No horse neither."

"He deserved it," Ned whispered, lowering

his smoking Colt to his side. "He was nothin' but a yellow bastard in the first place."

Slade looked back to the south. "Best we get our horses saddled and clear out of here. Morgan will be comin', after he heard that gun."

"Are you scared of him too?" Ned asked.

"I never met a man I was truly scared of," Slade replied, "but I've damn sure been in some places where I shouldn't have been, where I was at a big disadvantage. This creek is one of 'em, and I figure it's smart to get to a spot where we can defend ourselves."

Conrad's gagging distracted Ned. "One of you shut that kid up. Knock him out, or somethin'."

"I'll do it," Lyle said, moving over to the boy.

With the butt of his rifle, Lyle silenced Conrad Browning with one blow to his skull.

"We'll have to tie him over his horse," Lyle observed when Conrad lay still.

"It don't make a damn bit of difference to me," Ned answered quickly. "Get our horses ready. We're clearing out of here for Gypsum Gap."

"Suits the hell out of me," Slade muttered as he started toward the picket ropes. "I've never been so damn cold in my life."

Ned gave their back trail a look. "You bastard, Morgan," he hissed, holstering his pistol.

In a matter of minutes they had Conrad tied over his saddle and begun moving out.

Billy Miller lay dead by the smoldering remains of their campfire.

"Three of them," Frank whispered.

Tin Pan nodded.

"They've got Conrad roped to a horse."

"Appears he's out cold," Tin Pan said. "Or he could be dead as a fence post."

"Ned Pine won't kill him yet."

"What makes you so damn sure?"

"Ned wants me. He knows I'll keep following him until we get to the right place where he thinks he has the advantage over me."

"What are you gonna do, Morgan?"

"I'll stay with them every step of the way. If I get a chance to kill the others, I will."

"You're taking a big chance that Pine will kill your son, ain't you?"

"Not if I do it right."

"I've never met a man who was so dead set on one thing like your are."

"Did you ever have a son?"

Tin Pan nodded. "A long time ago. His mother didn't think I was fit to raise him, so she moved off to Baltimore and I never saw the boy again."

Frank stood up behind the pine tree on a ridge above the dry stream where they'd been watching Ned, and what was left of his gang, pull out. "I had the same problem. Vivian, Conrad's mother, took him away from me when her father ordered her to do it. Conrad and I scarcely know each other, and he resents me for not being there when he was younger."

"Does he know the whole story?"

"No."

"How come you don't tell him?"

"I never had the chance...until now."

Tin Pan squinted into the snow. "There's an old mining town northwest of here. I think it was called Gypsum Gap. That was the town you mentioned."

"That boy who rode with Ned told me."

"I can find it."

"I'm staying close to Pine, and my son. Wherever they go, that's where I'm going."

"You're a hardheaded cuss."

"Maybe I am." Frank sighed, heading off the ridge to their horses.

"Ain't no maybe to it." Tin Pan chuckled.

"Looks like this snow will never let up," Frank said, to change the subject from himself.

"No doubt about it. That sky has got lead in it. We can count on bein' chilly for a spell."

Ned was riding out in front with Conrad tied over the saddle of a bay gelding. Lyle and Sloan covered their back trail as they made for Gypsum Gap.

"I say we cut and run," Lyle said softly to Sloan. "This is personal between Ned and Morgan. I can't see no way either one of us is gonna make a dime."

"I'm afraid you're right," Slade said. "We could starve to death waitin' for Ned to make up his mind to find a bank or a train we can rob."

"This snow will cover us...if we decide to leave Ned today," Lyle remarked.

"I'm not worried about Ned."

"He's dangerous, Slade. He might decide to come after us if we leave."

"I'm not worried. I'll kill the son of a bitch if he tries to stop us."

"Maybe we oughta just shoot him now...in the back, and get the hell away from here."

"It'd be easy," Slade agreed.

"I can draw a bead on him and blow his guts out the front of his belly right now."

Slade looked behind them. The road was clear for a quarter of a mile. "Let's wait," he said. "I've had a look at Ned's poke. It's full of gold coins. If we're gonna kill the son of a bitch, we may as well rob him."

"He's carryin' gold?"

"Lots of it. I seen it myself back in town when he paid for the whiskey."

"How much you figure?"

"A leather pouch bigger'n my fist packed with gold coins and paper money."

"Jesus."

"But he's real careful with it. It was an accident when I saw him draw it out...he didn't know I was standing behind him looking."

"I say we kill him and take the gold," Lyle said with more than a little conviction.

"We've gotta choose the right time for it, and just the right place," Slade warned. "He's quick with a six-shooter, and if he knows what we're about to do, he'll pull iron and we'll be in one helluva fight."

"I know he's good," Lyle said, "but he can't be good enough to take both of us."

Slade turned in the saddle. The roadway was still clear behind them. "I'd have said the same thing about this Frank Morgan, only he's killed off our bunch one or two at a time and we're in a fix."

"You just give the word," Lyle said.

"The right time will come," Slade assured him.

"What's wrong with right now, Slade? I can pull my Winchester and drop him before you can sneeze."

"Don't be too damn sure of it."

"Are you losin' your nerve, Slade? That sure as hell ain't like you."

"I'm being smart. And careful."

Ned turned his horse up a steep part of the road with Conrad's horse tied to his saddle horn.

"I swear I can kill him now," Lyle insisted.

"Wait," was all Slade said.

"I was only thinkin' about that money pouch."

"It'll still be in his pocket no matter when we decide to kill him."

Lyle glanced backward. "Morgan will hear the shots when we kill Ned. He'll come after us."

Slade shook his head. "All he wants is that crybaby boy of his. He don't know about Ned's gold. If we leave the kid alive, Morgan won't follow us."

Lyle looked down at his gloved hands. "It's creepy, how one man can kill so many people.

Ned keeps sayin' Morgan is old, that he's washed up."

"He don't seem all that washed up to me," Slade remarked as they started their horses up the climb. "What he is, is real damn careful."

"Maybe he was as good as his reputation," Lyle said.

"That ain't what's worryin' me," Slade told his partner. "I'm worried that he's still as good as they say he was."

Twenty-nine

Louis Pettigrew saw them a couple of hours after dawn. They were riding behind him on the far side of a yawning snow-covered valley, a gang of men numbering at least a dozen. They were headed in his direction.

He'd heard about outlaw gangs in this part of Colorado Territory, and something told him to get away from these men if he could.

He heeled the rented horse into a lope.

"It could be that gang they told me about at the Wagon Wheel Saloon," he said aloud, drumming his shoes into the horse's sides for all he was worth.

He wasn't thinking about Frank Morgan any longer, or the story he'd come here to write; just getting out of this part of Colorado Territory alive would be enough to satisfy him after finding out the truth regarding Morgan and his overblown reputation.

His horse galloped through the snow on an old mining road that had begun to climb into snow-clad mountains. He remembered the road from his ride down out of Denver before the late spring snowstorm hit.

"The things I agree to do just to get a story," he muttered softly.

He'd been to Africa and South America in search of news his readers wanted, but this trip to the Wild West had been an utter waste. Frank Morgan, one of the last living gunfighters, was a myth, a legend in the overactive imaginations of men with nothing else to talk about.

"Who the hell is that?" Tin Pan asked, watching a man in a derby hat riding hard in their direction. He only caught brief glimpses of the rider coming through the snow. It was an odd place to find anyone who was pushing a horse so hard. That spelled trouble in Tin Pan's experience.

"I've got no idea," Frank replied. "Whoever he is, he's in a hurry. Unusual in this weather."

"Maybe somebody's after him," Tin Pan suggested. "Sure does seem like it."

"Hard to say," Frank told the old trapper, squinting into the snowfall. "He's dressed like a city slicker. This is a real strange place to find a tinhorn, especially when the weather's this bad."

"And one that's in a hurry," Tin Pan

reminded him. "I was thinkin' the same thing."

"Yeah. I'll ride on ahead to keep an eye on Ned Pine and my boy. You stay back and watch this fellow. See what he's up to, and if anybody's after him. Maybe he's being followed. That would explain why he's riding so fast. There could be somebody behind him."

"Martha will tell me," Tin Pan said. "After he rides by this knob, if she keep lookin' southwest, I'll know there's somebody on his trail."

"I never met a man who put so much trust in a mule," Frank said with a grin.

Tin Pan gave him a sideways look. "You'll learn one of these days, son, if you stay alive long enough. A mule has got better instincts than any dog or any man. Better senses too. If you aim to stay in this high country, you'll get yourself a good mountain mule."

Frank was still grinning when he rode off to the north behind Ned and Conrad and the two remaining gunmen who were with Ned now.

Tin Pan stepped out from behind a tree with his rifle aimed at the man in the bowler. "Hold it right there, mister," he said in a loud voice.

The man jerked his winded horse to a halt and threw his hands in the air. "If you intend to rob me, sir, you'll be sorely disappointed. I'm not carrying any large amount of money, just a few dollars."

"I ain't no highwayman. You're gonna kill that horse if you keep runnin' him through these snowdrifts. You can lower them hands now."

The stranger let his palms drop to the top of his saddle horn, though he did it slowly.

"Speak up," Tin Pan demanded, still holding his rifle at the ready.

"There's an outlaw gang behind me. It may be a man by the name of Ned Pine. There are at least a dozen of them. They're following me. At least that's the way it appears. I was told this area had several outlaw gangs roaming about, and to be very careful to avoid them."

"Ned Pine ain't followin' you," Tin Pan declared. "He's in front of you, and my partner, Frank, is trailin' him into these here mountains."

"Could that be Frank Morgan?" the stranger asked.

"Maybe. What business is it of yours? How come you know his name?"

"I came out West, out here from Boston, to write a story about him. He was a gunfighter."

"He could be called that."

"Only, I found out he's a fraud. There is no story to write about him."

"A fraud?"

The man nodded. "I met some gentlemen in Cortez who know him and they told me all about him. He shoots his victims in the back, or murders them in their sleep. He isn't a real shootist at all."

"Who told you that, mister?"

The man glanced behind him before he spoke

again. "One was named Ford Peters. Mr. Peters knew Morgan from years back. Then another gentleman by the name of Vic Vanbergen told me the rest of the story, about how sneaky Frank Morgan was, and that he was a coward."

Tin Pan chuckled.

"What is so funny?"

"You've got several things mighty wrong," Tin Pan began as the humor left his face. "First off, Frank Morgan may be the quickest draw with a handgun this side of the whole Mississippi River."

"I was told otherwise," the stranger said. He sounded sure of it.

"You got bad information," Tin Pan continued. "But when you listened to Victor Vanbergen, you were hearin' from one of the leaders of the outlaw gangs you're so worried about. Him and ol' Ned Pine have robbed banks and trains all over. I don't know him personal, just by reputation, but he's a no-good cutthroat and a robber by profession. If you met him, you're lucky he didn't rob you."

"I didn't know..."

"Well, now you do."

"I'd heard from various lawmen that Frank Morgan was a real gunfighter, perhaps one of the last of his breed. My name is Louis Pettigrew. I'm with the *Boston Globe* and my readers are hungry for stories about real-life gunmen. But those men told me Morgan was a fake...that he wasn't a real gunfighter at all in the true sense of the word. They described him as a common murderer."

"Morgan's the real thing. You can print that if you take the notion. He's killed eight or nine of Ned Pine's outlaws and before it's all over, he'll kill the rest of 'em and most likely Ned Pine himself."

Pettigrew glanced over his shoulder. "My God," he mumbled softly. "The men I was talking to last night are outlaws and robbers?"

"Now you're gettin' the picture," Tin Pan told him. "Like I said, you're lucky you wasn't robbed yourself."

"Would Mr. Morgan grant me an interview so I can present his story to my readers?"

"Can't say for sure. One thing you can count on...he ain't talking to nobody until he gets his son back."

"His son?"

"Ned Pine is holding his boy for ransom. Morgan is after Ned to save his boy's life. He ain't just some cold-blooded killer."

Darker clouds scudded over the knob where Tin Pan was talking with Louis Pettigrew. The snowflakes grew thicker on gusts of wind.

"I'd like to talk to Mr. Morgan," Pettigrew said. "I'd like to tell our readers his side of the story."

"You'll have to wait until his business with Ned Pine is settled, that's for sure."

"May I ride along with you in order to meet him?" Pettigrew asked.

"Maybe. If you can do it quiet. I won't guarantee that Morgan will talk to you."

"I'll take that chance," Pettigrew said.

Tin Pan lowered the muzzle of his Sharps. "My name's Tin Pan. Clarence Rushing was what I was called back when I was a sight younger."

"Pleased to meet you, Mr. Rushing. Or Mr. Tin Pan."

"Tin Pan is what they call me. I used to pan for gold in these mountains."

"Did you find any?"

"Not a single flake of placer. I trap for furs now. It pays better. Ride that horse over this hill and I'll fetch my mule and a borrowed horse. We'll catch up to Morgan in a couple of hours...maybe less."

"What about those men behind me?"

Tin Pan chuckled. "Morgan will take care of Vanbergen and his gang, just like he did the bunch with Ned Pine. You've got a chance to give your readers back in Boston a first-hand account of how a gunfighter goes about his profession, if things go like I figure they will."

Ford Peters spoke to Vern. "This is the dumbest thing I've ever done. We ain't robbin' nobody. We're followin' Vic back to Gypsum Gap so we can freeze our asses off while Ned Pine gets his revenge against this Frank Morgan."

"We damn sure ain't makin' no money," Vern agreed as they rode at the back of Vic's gang.

"I say we light a shuck out of here and go back to Texas," Ford said.

"Vic will send the rest of the boys after us

247

if we run out on him. They'll hunt us down."

"If this snow gets any heavier, nobody'll know we're gone until we've got a few hours' lead time. We can make it, if we push our horses."

"It's taking a helluva chance."

"We take chances every time we rob a bank or hold up a train. We could get our heads blowed off, ridin' with Vanbergen."

"But we've got a chance to make some money while we take those chances," Ford said.

"We damn sure ain't got that chance here," Vern agreed.

"First chance we get, let's ride back," Ford suggested in a whisper.

"It makes sense."

"Snow's startin' to fall heavier. It'll make it easier for us to get away."

Vern swallowed, pulling his bandanna higher on his face to warm his nose and mouth. "I'm with you, Ford. Whenever you decide to light out of here, we'll ride like hell back to the south."

"Just give this snow a few more minutes. Hell, Vic won't know we're gone until we're halfway back to Cortez if this snow gets any worse."

"Maybe we hadn't oughta use this road," Vern wondered as they rounded a stand of trees.

"Only way to make good time. We spur these broncs until their flanks are bloody. We can steal fresh horses back in Cortez and make for the Texas panhandle, or head for the New Mexico Territory line."

"Suits the hell out of me," Vern said. "I've

never been so goddamn cold in my life, and as far as I can tell we're doing this for nothing."

"You've got that right. I'm flat busted, and Vic ain't showed no signs of wantin' to fill my pockets with a share of any bank loot."

"Let's pick our spot and disappear," Vern said. "I'll bet Al and Todd will go with us."

Ford nodded. "Ride up there an' talk to 'em. But be sure you pull 'em off to one side. If Vic finds out what we're planning to do, he'll start shooting at us. Some of the others will side with him too."

Vern urged his horse up to the rear of the bunch and motioned Al, then Todd, off the trail. The others didn't seem to pay any attention to what Vern was doing.

The three men held a short conversation; then Vern trotted his horse back to Ford.

"They're ready to pull stakes whenever we are," Vern said through his ice-covered bandanna.

"Now's as good a time as any," Ford said.

Four riders peeled away from the rear of Victor Vanbergen's gang. They struck a lope toward the south, glancing over their shoulders until they were half a mile away.

"We done it," Vern said to the rest of the men. "Vic won't send anybody after us now, an' by the time he notices we're gone, this snow will have covered our tracks."

Thirty

Two hours of following Ned and his men through dense forests along a winding road had put an edge on Frank's nerves. The pair of gunmen at the rear had fallen back about a hundred yards, and they seemed to be talking softly to each other. Frank wondered about them, why they were dropping farther back. Were they planning to run out on Ned?

"Time I made my move," Frank said, tying off his horses in a pine grove. On foot, he approached a turn in the road where the two outlaws would be out of Ned's line of vision for a short time.

He was taking a huge risk. Gunshots might force Ned to shoot Conrad. But the boy was lashed over his saddle and by all appearances, he was unconscious...perhaps even dead. It was a gamble worth taking.

Frank slipped up to a thick ponderosa trunk where the road made a bend. He opened his coat and swept his coattails behind the butts of his twin Peacemakers.

When the distance was right, he stepped out from behind the tree to face the gunmen.

"Howdy, boys," he said, bracing himself for what he knew would follow. "You've got two choices. Toss your guns down and ride back wherever you came from, or go for those pistols. It don't make a damn bit of difference to me either way. I'd just as soon kill you as allow you to ride off."

"Morgan!" one of the riders spat.

"You've got my name right."

Before another word was said the second outlaw clawed for his six-shooter. Frank jerked his right-hand Colt and fired into the gunman's chest.

The man was knocked backward out of his saddle when his horse spooked at the sound of gunfire, tossing its rider over the cantle of his saddle into the snow as the sorrel gelding ran off into the trees.

But it was the second man Frank was aiming at now, as the fool made his own play.

Frank fired a second shot. His bullet struck the outlaw in the head, twisting it sideways on his neck as he slumped over his horse's withers. When the bay wheeled to get away from the loud noise, the gunman toppled to the ground. Blood spread over the snow beneath his head.

The bay galloped off, trailing its reins.

Frank walked over to both men. One was dead, and the other was dying.

With no time to waste, Frank took off at a run to collect his horse to go after Ned Pine. The only thing that mattered now was saving Conrad's life...if the boy wasn't already dead, or seriously injured.

Pine heard Frank's horse galloping toward him from the rear and he looked over his shoulder, reaching inside his coat for his pistol. Frank had to make a dangerous shot at long range before Ned put a bullet in Conrad.

Frank aimed and fired, knowing it would take a stroke of luck to hit Pine. But the fates were with Frank today when the horse Conrad was riding tried to shy away, breaking its reins, dashing off into the trees with the boy roped to the seat of its saddle.

Frank knew he had missed Pine, even though the bullet had been close. Pine spurred his horse, firing three shots over his shoulder as he galloped off in another direction, continuing northward.

Frank understood what he had to do. Finding out about his son's condition was more important than chasing down a ruthless outlaw. There would be plenty of time for that later, after he got Conrad to safety.

"We'll meet again somewhere, Pine," he growled as he reined into the trees to follow Conrad's horse.

Moments later, he found his son. Jumping down from the saddle, he ran over to him.

"Are you okay, Conrad?"

Conrad blinked. "My head hurts. One of them hit me." Then he gave Frank a cold stare. "What are you doing here? Why did you come?"

"I came to get you back," Frank replied as he began unfastening the lariat rope holding Conrad across the saddle. He pulled out his knife and cut the ropes binding Conrad's wrists and ankles.

Conrad slid to the ground on uncertain legs, requiring a moment to gain his balance. "How come you were never there when I was growing up, Frank Morgan?" he asked, a deep scowl on his face. "I wish the hell you'd never come here."

"It's a long story. I'm surprised your mother didn't tell you more about it. It had to do with her father. And I was framed for something I didn't do."

"Save your words," Conrad said, rubbing his sore wrists. "I don't ever want to see you again the rest of my life. You mean nothing to me."

Frank's heart sank, but he knew he'd done the only thing he could.

He was distracted by the sounds of horses coming down a hill above the road. Frank reached for a pistol, until he recognized Tin Pan and his mule, although someone else, the man they'd seen earlier in the derby hat, was riding with him.

Tin Pan and the stranger rode up.

"Nice shootin', Morgan," Tin Pan said. "We saw it from up that slope when you gunned down those two toughs. Couldn't get down in time to help you, although it didn't appear you needed any help."

"I saw the whole thing," the stranger said. "You're every bit as fast as they say you are. You killed two men, and you made it look easy."

Tin Pan chuckled, giving Conrad a looking over before he spoke. "This here's Mr. Louis Pettigrew from the *Boston Globe*, Morgan. He came all the way to Colorado Territory to get an interview with you."

"You picked a helluva bad time, Mr. Pettigrew," Frank said quickly. "Right now, I'm taking my son back to Durango. He's been through a rough time and he may need to see a doctor. He has a gash on top of his head."

Conrad stiffened. "Don't ever call me your son again, Mr. Frank Morgan. You never were a father to me."

Frank shrugged. "Suit yourself, Conrad. Maybe, after you've had time to think about it, we can talk about what happened back when you were born. It'll take some time to explain."

"I'd rather not hear it," Conrad said, sulking. "You weren't there when I needed you, and that's all that mattered to me, or my late mother."

Tin Pan gave Frank a piercing stare. "Sounds like you shoulda left this ungrateful boy tied to this horse while Ned Pine took him to Gypsum Gap."

Frank didn't care to talk about it with a stranger. "What about Vic Vanbergen and his bunch? Have you seen any sign of them on this road."

"Sure did," Tin Pan replied, "only some of 'em turned back and took off at a high lope. He ain't got but maybe half a dozen men with him now, but we're liable to run into 'em on the trail back south. There could be trouble."

"I can handle trouble," Frank remarked, stalking off to get his saddle horse and packhorse with Conrad's harsh words still ringing in his ears.

"I never knew anyone could be so fast with a pistol," Louis Pettigrew said. "But I saw it with my own two eyes. What a story this will make!"

Frank ignored the newsman's remark. There was another story that needed to be told, in detail, to his son. Apparently, Conrad didn't know the truth about why Frank had to leave his beloved Vivian.

Frank mounted up and rode back to the trail. Conrad was still struggling to mount the outlaw's horse.

"Let's head southwest," Frank said. "I'll ride out front to be sure this road is clear."

"We'll be right behind you," Tin Pan declared.

Conrad Browning did not say a word as they left the scene of his rescue.

Seven mounted men were crossing a creek at the bottom of a draw when Frank, Tin Pan, Pettigrew, and Conrad came to the crest of a rise.

"That's Vanbergen," Louis Pettigrew said. "He's the one who told me all those false tales about you."

Frank stepped off his horse with his Winchester .44-.40, levering a shell into the firing chamber. "I'll warm them up a little bit," he said. "You boys pull back behind this ridge. I'm gonna pump some lead at 'em."

"The one in the gray hat is Vanbergen," Pettigrew said as he turned his horse.

"I know who Victor Vanbergen is," Frank growled.

Frank aimed for Vanbergen as his horse plunged across the shallow stream.

"Good to see you again, Vic," Frank whispered, triggering off a well-placed shot, jacking another round into the firing chamber as the roar of his rifle filled the draw.

Vanbergen's body jerked. He bent forward and grabbed his belly, but before Frank could draw another careful bead on him, he spurred his horse into some trees on the east bank of the creek.

The other gunmen wheeled their horses in all directions and took off at a hard run. One rider fired a harmless shot over his shoulder before he went out of sight on the far side of the dry wash.

"I got him," Frank said, searching the trees for Vanbergen as gun smoke cleared away from his rifle.

But to Frank's regret he saw Vanbergen galloping his horse over a tree-studded ridge, aiming due north. Seconds later he was out of sight.

"I'll find you one of these days, Vic," Frank said, grinding his teeth together. "Right now, I've got more important business with a doctor to see if my boy's okay."

He strode back over the ridge and swung up in the saddle, booting his rifle.

"Did you get any of 'em?" Tin Pan asked.

"I shot Vanbergen in the belly. If Lady Luck is with me, he's gut-shot and he'll bleed to death. But if he's still alive, one of these days I'll find him and settle this score for good."

Conrad glowered at Frank. "Mom was right. You're nothing but a killer."

"There were circumstances back then," Frank explained. "If you give me the chance, I'll tell you about them."

"I don't want to hear a damn thing you have to say, Frank. The only thing I want is for you to leave me alone."

Frank tried to push the boy's remarks from his mind. The kid couldn't know what he'd been through back when Vivian was alive, or what her father had done to him.

A time would come when Frank would get the chance to tell his side of the story. In the meantime, he'd take the boy back to Durango and let a doctor check him over.

Then there was other unfinished business to attend to when he got back, and the thought of it brought a slight smile to his rugged face.

Dog would be waiting for him. And Jeff. Frank had a future if he made the most of it. He only hoped that one of these days Conrad would come around. At least listen to his side of the story.

"I hope you'll grant me the time for an interview," Louis Pettigrew said.

"We'll see," Frank replied. "It depends..."

Thirty-one

Doc Green finished putting the last stitch in Conrad's head and put his needle and sutures away. "It'll take a while to heal up right," the doctor said. "But you'll mend. Take a swallow of that laudanum when your head hurts."

Conrad nodded, stepping off the table in the doctor's office before giving Frank a look.

"Sorry this happened, Conrad," Frank said. "Ned Pine and Vic Vanbergen were out to get me. Wish you hadn't been the one to suffer for it."

They walked out on the doctor's front porch before Conrad said a word. "I'm grateful for what you did, Frank, but that won't make up for the years when you weren't there for me and my mother."

Frank stared down at his boots. "I take it Vivian didn't tell you the whole story?"

"The whole story? What else is there to say? You left us alone. You left her to raise me by herself."

"That isn't quite how it happened, and I can prove it if you'll listen to me."

"I don't want to hear a damn thing you have to say. Just leave me alone. You're nothing but a killer, a paid assassin. Mom told me that much, and so did my grandpa."

Frank let his gaze wander across the rooftops of Durango for a spell. "It's true that I've killed a few men. I'm not proud of it. But I didn't leave you and your mother because I wanted to. I didn't have a choice. I was framed for a crime I didn't commit. I didn't have any choice but to leave both of you, and I've regretted it every day of my life since."

"A likely story."

"It's the truth. If you'll allow it, one of these days I'd like to tell you about it. Then you can make up your own mind about who's telling the truth."

"Mom wouldn't lie to me," Conrad insisted.

"There were things she probably couldn't tell you. All I want is a chance for you to listen to me. Your grandfather had it in for me. He put me on the run and there was no way I could prove I was innocent."

"Just leave me alone, Frank. And don't ever call me your son again."

Frank went down the steps to his horse. "All I want you to do is hear what I have to say about what happened. I don't see how that's asking too much."

Conrad turned to head down the boardwalk. Then he stopped. "Maybe I do owe you that much, but I'll have to have some time to think about it."

"That's all I'm asking."

"We'll see," Conrad told him. "Right now all I want to do is get you out of my sight. I suppose I should be grateful that you got me away from Ned Pine and his hoodlums, but I've had too many years to think about how you abandoned me and my mother. I don't want to think about it now."

"I understand," Frank said quietly.

He mounted his horse as Conrad marched away. Frank's heart was heavy with sorrow. If the boy only knew the whole truth, he might take a different view of things.

He swung his horse away from the hitch rail, heading out to see about Dog and Jeff. He had plans to make.

Just once, he looked up at the mountains where he had tangled with Ned Pine and Victor Vanbergen.

"I'll be back up there one of these days," he promised himself. "And when I do, things won't go so easy on either one of you."

Frank led his packhorse down the street, but he drew up short when Louis Pettigrew came off the steps of the hotel.

"Mr. Morgan," Pettigrew began, "I was hoping you'd have time to talk to me."

"Not now," Frank replied. "I've got some things weighing heavy on my mind."

"Would tomorrow be okay?"

"A day or two," Frank told him. "Right now, I've got a dog to check on, and a young friend waiting for me."

Pettigrew nodded. "Just remember that I would very much like to give my readers the true story of Frank Morgan, the gunfighter," he said.

"I'm not a gunfighter anymore," Frank answered. "Just a man who's trying to live peaceful, if folks will let me."